Patchwork Connections

a quilting cozy

Carol Dean Jones

T0163138

C&T PUBLISHING
Another Maker Inspired!

Text copyright © 2018 by
Carol Dean Jones

Photography and artwork copyright ©
2018 by C&T Publishing, Inc.

Publisher: Amy Marson

Creative Director: Gailen Runge

Acquisitions Editor: Roxane Cerda

Managing Editor: Liz Aneloski

Project Writer: Teresa Stroin

Technical Editor / Illustrator:
Linda Johnson

Cover/Book Designer: April Mostek

Production Coordinator: Tim Manibusan

Production Editor: Alice Mace Nakanishi

Photo Assistant: Mai Yong Vang

Cover photography by Lucy Glover and
Mai Yong Vang of C&T Publishing, Inc.

Cover quilt: *Memories of Home*, 2014,
by the author

Published by C&T Publishing, Inc.,
P.O. Box 1456, Lafayette, CA 94549

Library of Congress Cataloging-in-
Publication Data

Names: Jones, Carol Dean, author.

Title: Patchwork connections : a quilting
cozy / Carol Dean Jones.

Description: Lafayette, California :
C&T Publishing, [2018] | Series:
Quilting cozy series ; book 4

Identifiers: LCCN 2018003703 |
ISBN 9781617457463 (softcover)

Subjects: LCSH: Quilting--
Fiction. | Retirees--Fiction. |
Retirement communities--Fiction. |
Interpersonal relations--Fiction. |
GSAFD: Mystery fiction.

Classification: LCC PS3610.O6224 P38
2018 | DDC 813/.6--dc23

LC record available at
https://lccn.loc.gov/2018003703

POD Edition

A Quilting Cozy Series

by Carol Dean Jones

Tie Died (book 1)

Running Stitches (book 2)

Sea Bound (book 3)

Patchwork Connections (book 4)

Stitched Together (book 5)

Moon Over the Mountain (book 6)

The Rescue Quilt (book 7)

Missing Memories (book 8)

Tattered & Torn (book 9)

Left Holding the Bag (book 10)

Beneath Missouri Stars (book 11)

Frayed Edges (book 12)

Acknowledgments

My sincere appreciation goes out
to my special friends Phyllis Inscoe
and Janice Packard.

I thank each of you for the many
hours you spent reading and re-reading
these chapters, for bringing the plot
inconsistencies to my attention,
for finding the many errors that
were so arrogantly ignored by the
spelling software and especially for
providing the endless support that is
so needed in what could otherwise
be a very lonely task.

Prologue

Martha turned her headlights off and drove slowly past her house. The black car was parked across the street. There was no moon, but even in the dark of night, she recognized the car. It had been outside her house frequently over the past few weeks. It was sometimes in her office parking lot. Occasionally she would see it in her rearview mirror as she drove. She reported it to the police, but no laws had been broken. At least not yet.

She attempted to garner enough courage to stop and confront the driver, but fear held her back. As she passed the car, she could make out a shadowy figure and the red tip of a burning cigarette.

Martha turned left at the next corner and again into the alley behind her house. Trembling, she slipped out of the car and hurried into the house. She grabbed her phone to call the police but went to the window and, as always, the car was gone.

She hung up without dialing. Again.

Chapter 1

"I can't possibly manage the shop while you're away, Ruth! I know nothing about running a quilt shop!" Sarah exclaimed.

"Sarah!" Ruth retorted. "You managed the largest grocery store in Middletown for years! It's no different. And you'll have help! Anna and Geoff do all the online sales, and she'll take care of the inventory. I'm sure Anna can spend a few hours with you in the shop when you need her, and you can close at night until I come back if you want. Please think about it," Ruth pleaded.

Sarah walked around the quilt shop wondering what it would be like to work there. She knew what her hesitation was, but she didn't tell Ruth. Sarah had only been quilting for a couple of years, and she often heard customers asking Ruth questions she would never be able to answer. She wanted to talk about that with Ruth, but she was embarrassed. She knew Ruth would assure her she could handle it, but when it came to quilting, Ruth had far more confidence in her than she had in herself.

She loved being in the shop. There were quilts hanging on every available wall, and the bolts displayed a dazzling rainbow of color when customers stepped into the shop.

"What about the classes?" Sarah asked. "I can't teach classes."

"We can postpone the winter classes, or I can try to find a teacher to come in. Actually, I was wondering if you might want to teach one of the classes you took on the quilting cruise." Sarah had just returned from an exciting Caribbean quilting cruise.

"*Me?*" Sarah wailed. "I'm no teacher."

"I think you would be a great teacher, Sarah, but right now I need you in the shop."

"Let me get back to you tomorrow, Ruth. I know you need to make your plans, so I'll decide quickly. By the way, how's your mother? Have you heard anything?"

"She doesn't have long. She's insisted on staying at home, and I guess that's best. All the hospital can do is prolong her life, and she's ready to go. Papa wanted to be at home, too, but he died in the hospital. That must have felt so alien to him," she added sadly.

Ruth was born Amish and lived in Ohio until she was seventeen. She went away to art school during her *rumspringa*, that time that Amish young people spend outside of their community to make sure they are ready to commit to the Amish way of life. While away, she met Nathan and they were married. Ruth's father rejected them both and, for many years, Ruth lived outside her community and away from her family.

Ruth's mother was not as adamant about it, and now that her husband was gone, she wanted to spend her last days with Ruth, perhaps to make up for lost years.

"I could ask Katie to take a semester off and come work in the shop, but she's doing so well! I just can't bring myself to do that to her."

"Absolutely not, Ruth! Don't do that. Your daughter is exactly where she should be. We'll work this out some way. I want to talk with Charles, and I'll call you in the morning."

"Thank you, Sarah," Ruth said as she hugged her friend. "I appreciate that you would even consider it. I'll talk to you tomorrow."

Sarah left the shop and returned home through the park. It was a cool October afternoon with a bite in the air. She wished she had brought Barney. He loved walking into town, and he was such good company. *If he were with me now, I'd talk this over with him, and he would look at me with his big brown eyes full of love and wag his tail.* Sarah adopted Barney from the Humane Society when she first moved to Cunningham Village. He helped her adjust to life in a retirement community by giving her love, an excuse to go out walking in the neighborhood, and someone to share her new life.

Arriving home, she scratched Barney's ears and opened the back door for him, again feeling thankful she had enclosed the backyard with a fence. She then put in a call to Charles. "How about dinner?" she asked when he answered. He agreed immediately, and they decided to drive into town for Chinese food. She had been seeing Charles for over a year, and it was becoming evident to both of them that this was much more than a friendship. Sarah was aware that Charles was in love with her, but she had been reluctant to face her own feelings. When she lost her husband, Jonathan, she had been devastated, and didn't expect to ever fall in love again. However, if she were honest with herself, she would have to admit that is precisely what had happened. At seventy years old, she was in love!

"Let's go see Sophie," she said to Barney. He jumped up from his spot in the kitchen and ran in a circle before clumsily pulling his leash off the hook and dropping it at Sarah's feet. It wasn't that he understood all of what she said, but the word *go* was enough for him!

They walked across the street to Sophie's house, Barney sniffing the entire way. Despite her raucous personality, Sophie had been Sarah's closest friend and confidant since she moved to the village. Sophie was in her mid-seventies and rotund with a contagious laugh and an endless repertoire of hilarious stories. She also had a heart of gold and was the best friend a person could have.

"Don't bring that flea magnet into my house," Sophie said gruffly as she opened the door.

"Sophie! You know you don't mean that, and you've hurt his feelings!" Sarah responded as they followed her into the living room.

As soon as Sophie was seated, Barney hurried over and put his paws on her lap, looking lovingly into her eyes. She surreptitiously slipped a treat from her pocket, which he appeared to inhale before stretching out across her feet. "His feelings don't look hurt to me," Sophie grumbled. Barney closed his eyes and sighed deeply.

"I can see you managing Stitches," Sophie told Sarah after hearing about Ruth's dilemma, but she didn't have much sympathy for Sarah's fears. "I don't get it! You know how to quilt. You managed Keller's Market for years. Why not manage Running Stitches?"

"You make it sound so simple, Sophie. What if a customer asks me something I don't know?"

"Well, let me see now." Sophie scrunched up her face, held her head, and faked deep concentration for a few moments. She suddenly looked up with surprise and said, "I've got it! You say, 'I don't know!'"

"Oh, Sophie. I guess I'm just scared, and I shouldn't let that stop me."

"... and you could take Barney with you."

"Really?" Sarah responded, brightening up. She hadn't thought of that, but it would be fun having him there with her. Ruth had encouraged her to bring him anytime, and many of the customers had gotten to know him. "I would feel better with him there for some reason."

By the time Charles arrived that evening, Sarah had just about decided to take on the challenge. A few minutes with Charles concluded the debate. She had expected the evening to be about deciding what to do and, instead, it turned out to be a celebration of a new adventure.

Chapter 2

Sarah's daughter, Martha, was forty-three years old. She had been married briefly in her twenties but never discussed the reasons behind the breakup, at least not with Sarah. Martha and her mother were very different and, as a result, their relationship suffered over the years. Sarah, with her very positive outlook, enjoyed life and her friends. She was eager for new experiences and open to new ideas. Martha was more like her father who was a very serious-minded and hardworking man.

As a child, Martha had been quiet and somewhat withdrawn. She preferred books to people and, as a result, her grades were exceptional and her social skills nil. She graduated high school at sixteen and received her bachelor's degree at nineteen, followed immediately by her master's and her PhD. Sarah was never able to bridge the ever growing chasm between them.

Once Sarah moved into the retirement village, she rarely saw Martha. "She was adamant that I move here," Sarah told Charles one day when they were discussing family, "but now that I'm here, she seems to have forgotten me."

"That happens," Charles had responded. "Don't take it personally. Our kids have busy lives. They're building their careers and caring for their own families. They haven't forgotten us. They're just busy chasing squeaking wheels."

"Maybe I should squeak more," Sarah had responded, "but I doubt she would notice."

Martha had no family to care for, but she certainly was building her career. She had been working for the same firm for the past fifteen years. As a senior scientist, she was in charge of several contracts providing basic research for the pharmaceutical industry. She never shared the details of her work with the family, dismissing their questions by saying that her work was classified.

Sarah had expressed concern to Charles, hoping that being involved in classified projects didn't place her daughter in any danger. "More likely," Charles had responded, "the work is proprietary rather than classified. She probably just needs to avoid any opportunity for project details to be obtained by competitors."

Martha was a tall, attractive woman, but, unlike her fair-skinned mother, she had an olive complexion that she got from her father's side of the family. Her hair was brown and cropped short without a sign of gray. Her eyes were hazel and seemed to change with her moods. On the rare occasions that she was relaxed, gold flecks danced against a green background, but Sarah hadn't seen that sparkle for years. Most of the time, her eyes remained dark and determined.

Martha supervised a group of scientists, some young just out of school and others approaching retirement age. Her coworkers saw her as diligent, task-oriented, and precise. She didn't attract personal relationships and was seen as being without close friends. That's what made it so unusual that a man eight years her junior would become attracted to her. No doubt, her cool aloof manner fueled his obsession.

Derek Kettler had transferred into Martha's department, and less than a year later, she fired him for incompetence. Despite his glowing references and impressive resume, she found him to be unfocused and difficult. He rarely met deadlines and was argumentative when given assignments. If any of his objections had been of value, Martha would have given them consideration, but generally, his arguments were simply self-serving.

Martha was glad to see him leave her department for another reason, although she didn't dare verbalize it to anyone. He made her feel uncomfortable. She didn't like the way he looked at her or the way he always seemed to be nearby. He had a habit of asking her personal questions and attempting to engage her in conversations about things outside the office. One day as they were leaving a meeting, he cornered her and asked her to go for drinks after work. Although she thought she had made it very clear that the request was inappropriate, he asked again a week later.

A few months after firing him, Martha received a call from Derek at her home. She briefly wondered why he hadn't called her at work. As it turned out, he asked her to go to dinner with him. She refused, but he pleaded with her, saying he needed to apologize and explain his poor performance. She told him that nothing he said would change the outcome; his previous position had been filled. Derek adamantly insisted he was not trying to get his job back; he just wanted her to understand. Against her better judgment, she agreed to meet him at The Pelican on Riverside Drive.

The evening at The Pelican was pleasant enough. Derek told Martha about his recent divorce and the loss of contact with his children when his wife moved away. Martha was uncomfortable about the amount of private information he was sharing, feeling these things were too personal to be revealed to a relative stranger. She was yet to realize that he certainly didn't see her as a stranger. She remained quiet most of the evening just listening.

At the end of the evening, she reiterated that she could not reinstate him, and she thanked him for the meal. He had insisted on picking up the check. She said goodnight, but as she was turning to leave, he reached for her forearm and pulled her toward him, attempting to kiss her. Before she thought about what she was doing, she had slapped him across the face. It was an instinctive move, and she was immediately sorry. They were on a crowded sidewalk outside the restaurant and people stopped to look. He stared at her in disbelief with his hand covering his cheek. "That was a big mistake, lady," he said coldly.

"I apologize," she said hesitantly. "You startled me." Regaining her composer, she added, "… but the mistake was yours. This was certainly *not* a date, and we have *no* personal relationship. Touching me was most inappropriate." His eyes grew black as he stood rigid, staring at her. She felt a chill creep slowly up her spine.

"I need to go," she said as she turned and walked quickly toward her car. "Good night," she added as she reached for her keys. He didn't respond. She hoped he didn't see her hands shaking as she attempted to unlock the car door. She hoped she could get into the car before he moved toward her.

Once inside, she started the car and pulled away from the curb. By the time she reached the end of the block, she was aware of her growing anger coupled with a feeling of helplessness, a feeling she hadn't experienced for years. "That man is dangerous," she told herself as she headed for the safety of home.

* * * * *

Ruth was delighted that Sarah had decided to manage the shop. Sarah was the only person she was willing to trust with this responsibility. She was smart, levelheaded, and she was an experienced manager. If Sarah had refused, Ruth had already decided she would close the shop and just leave the online business running while she was away. Geoff and Anna could manage that part. But she didn't want to do that since her customers depended on her. Running Stitches was the only quilt shop in Middletown.

Ruth and Sarah met at the shop the next day so that Ruth could show her the basics. Toward the end of the day, they spent several hours going over the computerized accounting system Geoff, her sister Anna's husband, had developed for the shop. Ruth decided to leave at the end of the week, fearing that her mother might not live more than a few weeks. "Are you comfortable with what you've seen so far?" Ruth asked as she walked Sarah to the door.

"Yes, I'm comfortable," Sarah responded. "But I've been thinking that I might call my daughter, Martha, and see if she'd like to come into the shop occasionally on the weekends. I know that's the only time she has to herself, but I think it would be good for us to spend some time together."

"That's a terrific idea, Sarah. If she wants to work weekends, I'd be happy to pay her."

"No. I just want her to be here with me. Maybe I can get her interested in some hand stitching while she's in the shop. I would love to share this part of my life with her. ..."

"And," Ruth interjected, "perhaps she will share a part of her life with you!"

That would be a welcome change, Sarah thought, unaware of the danger that decision would bring into their lives.

Chapter 3

Alan Fitzgerald was in his mid-forties with a cute, boyish look. He reminded Martha of an actor she had become fascinated with when she was only twelve. She had gone to the movie theater in Middletown with her parents to see *Privileged*, perhaps the first movie with the handsome young British actor Hugh Grant. At forty-three, she still made a point of renting his movies whenever she had a chance. She wished she could be like the women he would fall in love with in these movies but knew she was somehow different.

Alan Fitzgerald had been hired to fill the position vacated by Derek Kettler. When Alan walked into the lab, Martha was aware of his smile and the dark curls loosely falling on his forehead. When he spoke, she expected to hear a British accent and was surprised to hear, instead, a touch of Texas twang. She was taken with this handsome man and caught herself wishing he weren't married. She immediately admonished herself for the thought and for dwelling on such superficiality.

Alan quickly learned the job and was a bright, efficient researcher. His reports were detailed and precise, exactly what Martha had hoped for in an assistant. He was even able to lessen her own load by quickly assuming many of the responsibilities she had been performing because she didn't have an assistant she could depend upon. After he had been there a few months, she actually left work at 5:00 p.m. one Friday afternoon, something she hadn't been able to do for several years. Walking out of the office, she felt like a burden had been lifted and a tentative smile crept across her face.

Not being in the mood to head straight home, Martha decided to call her mother. They hadn't talked for several weeks, maybe more. Martha wondered if her mother might want to go out to dinner. She thought it would be good for the two of them to sit down, have a drink, and just visit like friends. She never understood the distance that existed between them, yet she was aware how different they were. Her mother was quick to laugh and appeared to be enjoying life, although Martha found it hard to understand. Life seemed so difficult to her, so intense.

"Hello, Mother?"

"Martha! I'm so glad you called. I've been thinking about you."

They exchanged the usual polite conversation and finally Martha got to the point saying, "I was hoping you might be free to go out to dinner tonight. I got off early, well early for me, and I was hoping you hadn't made dinner plans."

"I would love that, Martha! I just got home from Stitches. ..."

"Stitches?" Martha repeated questioningly.

"Running Stitches, the quilt shop where I took my classes. I've been meeting with the owner this week and, wait! If we're going to have dinner together, I'll tell you all about it then. Shall I fix something here?"

"I was thinking it would be fun to go out." Martha thought it would be better for them to be in neutral territory so that, perhaps, they could meet as friends and avoid their parent-child patterns from years past. "How about I pick you up in a half hour?"

"Perfect! I'll see you then." Sarah hung up feeling pleased but puzzled. It was so unlike Martha. She hoped nothing was wrong.

Sarah hurried out the front door just as Martha pulled up. Martha admired her mother's ability to always look so fresh and healthy. Her short blond hair came just below her ears and was sprinkled with gray. She had maintained her figure throughout her life and had a snap to her walk, which pointed to years of healthy living. As she watched her approach the car, Martha wondered about her mother's relationship with Charles. She had met Charles the previous year and liked him, despite her apprehension about her mother dating. *Charles has been good for her*, she thought, taking in her mother's relaxed, happy smile.

"Hi, sweetie," Sarah said as she slid effortlessly into the passenger's seat. "Where to?"

"I was thinking we could go to that new seafood restaurant out on Route 39. I've heard great things about it."

"I would love that," she responded enthusiastically. They both felt a bit self-conscious at first, and conversation was somewhat stilted, but once they were seated in the restaurant, they both began to relax.

"Tell me about your cruise," Martha said. They had talked briefly right after Sarah returned from her quilting cruise, but Martha hadn't taken the time to hear the details. Sarah launched into the many stories she had to tell about the trip and Martha found it interesting. "I just might consider taking a cruise someday," she said thoughtfully.

"We just might consider taking a cruise *together* some day," Sarah said with a raised eyebrow and a tentative smile. They both sat quietly imagining, each in her own way, what that might be like. The waiter arrived with their drinks and shrimp cocktails. As they sipped their wine and enjoyed the fresh shrimp, they found themselves actually having a good time. "Where do you suppose they get fresh seafood in the middle of the country like this?" Sarah asked her very knowledgeable daughter.

"I imagine they truck the fish down from Lake Michigan. As for the shellfish, who knows. Maybe they fly it in from the coast." About that time, the waiter arrived with their meals. The two women sat for another hour, slowly savoring their food and enjoying their time together. They ordered coffee and a scrumptious dessert to share before deciding it was time to head home.

The two women were quiet on the ride to Cunningham Village, neither feeling a need to fill the empty space with chatter. They hesitantly hugged as Martha dropped her mother off, both realizing Martha had shed a bit of her armor.

On her way home, Martha thought about her mother's request that she spend some time at Stitches while she was managing the shop. As she listened to her mother's various responsibilities, Martha could tell she was concerned about the computerized accounting system. "I just hope I don't completely fowl up Ruth's finances," her mother had said. Sarah was comfortable with basic computer functions; she had learned to surf the internet and use the word processing and emailing applications, but the shop computer was another thing.

Martha offered to develop a manual recording system that her mother could use during the week. She told her mother that she would come to the shop on Saturdays and update the computer system from the manual records. Sarah had looked visibly relieved, and both women realized it would offer them a chance to get reacquainted.

Although Martha felt she had good reasons for distancing herself from her family over the past two decades, she also knew it hadn't been that difficult for her to do. Distancing came natural to her. She preferred her laboratory to the outside world and research to personal interactions. However, she had to admit that she was missing a large part of life.

As she drove home, Martha didn't notice the black car that pulled out behind her, nor did she notice that it remained at a distance until she arrived home.

Chapter 4

Sarah woke up early feeling both excited and apprehensive. It was Friday and her first day managing Stitches. It would be a long day with the Friday Night Quilters coming into the shop that night. She fixed a quick breakfast, straightened up the kitchen and clipped Barney's leash onto his collar. "Yes, we have a big adventure today," she said as she led him to the car.

Arriving at Stitches, Sarah turned into the alley that ran along the side of the shop. She parked where Ruth always parked, leaving the street parking for her customers. *My customers*, she thought with a smile. As she and Barney approached the shop, she saw a precisely printed sign on the door announcing the new hours: *OPEN 10–5*.

Sarah had assured Ruth she was comfortable with keeping the shop open in the evening, but Ruth had insisted on closing at 5:00. There had been several robberies in Middletown, and she was concerned for Sarah's safety. All of the robberies had been in the downtown area, and Sarah was not worried. Stitches was in the suburbs and surrounded by a settled community.

As she opened the door, she was struck by the beauty of the fabrics and felt excited as she approached a new line Ruth had just added. *Beautiful!* She thought as she ran her hand over the colorful bolts. It was only 9:00, and she had an hour to get ready for her first customers. She knew she didn't need to be there so early, but she was eager for her new adventure to begin.

Sarah went into the kitchenette and got the coffee pot started. She opened a bag of cookies and spread them out on a plate. She made sure all the lights were on, opened the safe and took out the cash box. She arranged the money in the cash register and sat down on the stool awaiting her first customer. She looked at the clock and saw that it was only 9:20. Barney had already found a corner and had curled up for his morning nap. "Hmm," she said aloud. "I guess I don't need to come in *this* early."

To pass time, she checked to make sure the door was locked and went into the stock room to look at the fabrics that were waiting to be added to the shop as bolts were emptied. She became engrossed in the array of colors and designs and began thinking about quilts she could make. She decided to rearrange the bolts so they would be easier to get to when she needed them. When she returned to the main shop, she was surprised to see it was now a few minutes before ten. She unlocked the door and noticed a bolt of blue batiks out of place. As she was pulling the bolt out to move it, she heard the tinkle of the bell on the door. *My first customer!*

Sarah turned and was delighted to see Charles' smiling face as he came through the door. Barney jumped up to greet him, and Charles squatted down to allow the kisses Barney was so eager to bestow. "I tried to be your first customer," he said with a big grin as he walked toward her. "I guess I made it." They hugged and he kissed her gently.

She sent him into the kitchenette to get them both coffee and cookies and they spent the next half hour talking about the shop. He loved seeing the glitter in her eyes as she talked with excitement. *I'm glad Ruth left my girl in charge*, he thought. *This is making her very happy.*

At precisely 10:30, the bell tingled a second time. Sarah looked up eagerly to see her first *real* customers. Kimberly and Christina came rushing in, their eyes as big as saucers. "Sarah! What are you doing behind the register?" Obviously, Ruth hadn't had time to let everyone know she would be away. Kimberly and Christina were sisters and were part of the Friday Night Quilters, a group of friends that met in the shop to sew, show off their projects, and generally support one another. They had also purchased a long-arm quilting machine the previous year and did all of Sarah's quilting.

Sarah caught them up on what was happening with Ruth and asked if she could help them with anything, hoping they would say no. Fortunately, Kimberly spoke up saying, "We know exactly what we want! Ruth has a new line of very brightly colored modernistic fabrics, and I want to make a wall hanging for an artist friend of mine."

"That sounds like a perfect choice," Sarah responded. She knew the fabric line and led the two sisters right to it. Charles smiled from the sidelines, knowing about her fear of not knowing the answers. Sarah cut the fabric and rang up the sales without a hitch, considering her hands were shaking uncontrollably. She hugged them both as they left but called after them saying, "Are you two coming to the club meeting tonight?"

Christina looked surprised. "Are we going to be meeting with Ruth away?"

"I don't see any reason why we shouldn't. Maybe I should call everyone and make sure they know we're *on* for tonight."

"Sarah, I have everyone's number on that list Ruth made up for us. How about I do that for you in case you get busy?"

"Thank you, Christina. That would be great! I'll see you tonight."

As she waved to the sisters and closed the door, Charles asked with a look of concern, "What's this about tonight? I thought you weren't going to be working at night."

"Actually, Ruth and I never really resolved what to do about the Friday night group. At one point, she suggested that Anna might be able to be in charge of it, but she didn't get back to me. We both just forgot about it, I guess. I think we should go ahead and meet though. That get-together is important to the whole group!"

"Do you want me to come with you tonight?"

"Thank you, Charles, but I'll be fine." Charles walked a tight line with Sarah around issues involving her independent nature. His impulse was to be her protector, but she often saw that as smothering. She had an independent streak that was hard for him to understand after many years of being married to a woman who enjoyed being looked after. Of course, his wife had been sick, and Sarah was a healthy, vital woman eager to take care of herself. He let the subject drop, but it was difficult for him.

As he was getting ready to leave, Charles asked, "Would you like for me to take Barney for a walk before I go?"

"Oh my! That's something I completely forgot about. I can't leave the shop to take him outside. Would you please?"

The two returned a half hour later, and Charles saw that there were several groups of women busily pulling bolts down and asking Sarah's advice. He was pleased to see she was chatting away, pointing toward other bolts, and appearing to be completely comfortable in her new role. He smiled to himself and threw her a goodbye kiss when he caught her eye.

A couple of hours later, Sarah realized she was getting hungry. "That's another thing I forgot to plan for," she said aloud to no one. She called the café across the street and ordered a sandwich. Meanwhile, she made a sign to hang on the door saying she would be right back. She locked the door, hung the sign, and crossed the street with Barney in tow. She tied his leash to the newspaper dispenser outside the café and went in to pick up her lunch while keeping a close eye on the shop.

Later in the afternoon, the shop began to fill up with customers. Sarah could barely keep up with cutting fabric, ringing up sales, and explaining why Ruth wasn't there. She was thrilled to see Anna crossing the street heading for the shop. "Anna! I'm so glad to see you," she gushed as Anna entered the shop.

"I was thinking you might need me," Anna responded. "Fridays can be very busy. Geoff told me that two online orders came in today, and I came over to get those in the mail, but I can stay if you need me." Anna was Ruth's sister. They had been estranged for many years due to their father's strong Amish beliefs. After their father's death and when they were expecting their first child, Anna and her husband, craving a family connection, moved to Middletown to be near Ruth and her daughter, Katie. Geoff, a computer consultant, offered to set up an online shop for Ruth. Anna worked in the shop until Annabelle was born and afterward continued to process the online sales.

As predicted, the shop was busy all afternoon. Sarah and Anna worked together, keeping up with the customers and getting the online orders packaged up. With a deep sigh, they locked the door at precisely 5:00. As they were leaving, Sarah asked, "Are you planning to come to the club meeting tonight?"

Anna looked confused by the question, and said, "Ruth asked me to run the meeting on Friday nights. Has that changed?"

"No! It's just that Ruth forgot to get back with me about it. She said she was going to ask you, but she never let me know what you said. I'm delighted that you are going to do it! I'm feeling just a bit overwhelmed."

Anna reached into her pocket and pulled out a scrap of paper. "Take my number. Friday and Saturday afternoons can get very busy. Just give me a call and I'll pop over. In fact, anytime you need me, call. Geoff is working from home and Annabelle loves sitting in her bouncy chair next to him at the computer. She's daddy's little girl." Changing the subject, Anna asked, "Will you be coming tonight?"

"Absolutely! I'm going to relax with a hot bath, eat some dinner, and I'll be ready for the meeting by 7:00." The two women hugged, and Sarah headed for her car with Barney trotting along by her side.

"That was an excellent day!" she said to Barney as they drove home. He smiled and wagged his tail enthusiastically.

Chapter 5

Over the next two weeks, Sarah settled into running the shop as if she had done it for years. Her worries were unfounded in that either she knew the answers to her customers' questions, or they would figure the problems out together. She was having a fantastic time and was thinking about asking Ruth if she could work part time after she returned.

Martha came in for a few hours on the first two Saturdays, and they worked on the temporary account system she had developed. Sarah was able to keep track of the various data pieces on paper during the week, and Martha entered it all on the computer when she came in. "Ruth will be overjoyed," Sarah had told Martha when the first entries were completed, and a sample report had been run. "She expected to have this whole thing to sort out when she returned."

"How's her mother?" Martha asked. Sarah told her that her mother was barely conscious, and Ruth felt she needed to be in the hospital, but of course, she was honoring her mother's wishes to remain at home. The doctor had been visiting as was common in the Amish community, and she was being kept comfortable. Ruth called every few days with updates so Sarah could respond to the customers who were asking about her.

Martha and Sarah's relationship was improving. Now that they had a common interest around which to relate, they seemed to be getting closer. They had a particularly meaningful experience one Saturday when they encountered unexpected demands at Stitches.

Sarah had invited Martha to come for dinner after work that day. She had put a pot roast meal in the Crock-Pot, and they were looking forward to a relaxing evening. It was Saturday and, again, was a very busy day. Anna had come in for a few hours in the early afternoon but, once she left, a busload of quilters had stopped at the shop on their way to Hamilton. Renee, who was clearly the leader of the group, said that she had told Ruth the previous month that they would be there. Ruth had promised a special reception for them. Obviously, Ruth had forgotten to share this information with Sarah.

"I'm sorry, Renee," Sarah apologized. "Ruth had a family emergency and I'm sure your visit slipped through the cracks. But we can certainly make this work!" She asked Martha to hurry across the street to the café and purchase refreshments and, turning to the busload of women, she announced a 25% sale effective immediately. The group was overjoyed, and twenty-five or thirty women crowded into the shop. Martha returned with a tray of assorted sweets and hurried into the small kitchen to make coffee.

It was a very busy afternoon, with Sarah cutting fabric and Martha running the cash register nonstop. When the bus pulled away, Sarah took a deep breath and with a chuckle said, "Well, that was really exciting!"

"Exciting!" Martha exclaimed. "It was exhilarating! I had no idea selling fabric could be such fun!"

Sarah wondered if Martha had any idea why she had found the afternoon so rewarding. Earlier, Sarah had watched her laughing with customers and basking in the comradery that develops as quilters excitedly plan their creations. *This is a whole new world for her*, Sarah told herself with a smile.

"I enjoyed it too. Ruth's customers are such fun, creative people; they are a joy to be around!"

Once the bolts were returned to their proper shelves and the accessory wall organized, the two women began preparing to close. "I'm exhausted," Martha said as she pulled on her boots.

"Are you still having dinner with me tonight?"

"Of course!" Martha responded. "I wouldn't miss it! That'll be a relaxing end to a very busy day. Is Charles coming to dinner?"

"No. I wanted tonight to be just you and me. I was hoping we could talk." Martha smiled a nervous smile and dropped her eyes. She knew her mother wanted to talk about the past years. Martha had been distant from the whole family, and she knew she owed them an explanation. She just wasn't ready to talk about it. *Not yet anyway.* Sarah interrupted her daughter's thoughts just then by adding, "If you get home before I do, would you let Barney out? He's been alone since nine this morning."

The two women got into their respective cars. Martha turned and waved as she drove off. Sarah sat for a few minutes thinking about her daughter. It had been an incredible day, working closely with her on a shared activity. It was the kind of day she had always wanted to experience with her daughter, but Martha had always been too busy with her studies or too busy with her work. *Always too busy.*

When Sarah got home, Martha wasn't there but neither was Barney. The leash was gone, and Sarah figured they took off for the park? They both seemed to enjoy time spent together there. When Martha returned, Sarah was surprised to see a change in her demeanor. She seemed troubled.

"Martha, are you okay? Did something happen?"

"No, mother. I just had such a good time today, and it made me think of all the years I've been away from the family and all that I've missed."

"I know. It's bothered me too. Is it something I've done?"

Martha slumped down in a chair at the kitchen table and, much to her mother's surprise, tears began to form in her daughter's eyes. Sarah reached for the tissues and sat the box in front of Martha. Martha didn't move to blot the tears and, as she looked down, a tear slowly slid down her cheek. Martha shook her head slowly and removed a tissue from the box.

"It's not you, Mother. It was never you." They sat in silence for a while, Sarah hoping her daughter would continue.

Martha had been a quiet child. She never seemed to enjoy family functions and had very few friends. She would rather curl up in the sunroom with a book than to do most anything else. She didn't date much during her high school years, despite being a very pretty girl who was pursued by several young boys. Her weekends were often spent in the library, researching subjects that caught her eye.

In 1987 at the age of sixteen, Martha went away to college and graduated summa cum laude. Sarah and Martha's father, Jonathan, flew to California for her graduation but returned the next day as Martha had interviews scheduled for the rest of the week, and her parents felt they would be in the way.

Martha remained in California, accepting a job at the science department of the university and continuing with her graduate studies, ultimately obtaining her PhD. After graduation, she decided to take a road trip alone to "clear the cobwebs," as she said. She drove to northern Utah and then south through Utah's national parks. She called Sarah occasionally to describe the miraculous views and promised to send pictures as soon as she returned home.

While in Bryce Canyon, she met Greyson. Greyson, reportedly, was attending graduate school in Seattle. Martha called Sarah and was brimming over with excitement. She was in love! One month later, the couple was married. Sarah was worried about her. "So little experience in the real world," she had said to Jonathan.

No one was invited to the wedding, and the new couple moved immediately to Montana where Greyson reported having family. He never returned to Seattle or to his studies. Martha's calls became less frequent. Sarah continued to call, but Martha rarely had much to say. She was working and was too busy to talk or take time off to visit. When they did talk, Martha's voice was stilted.

In 1994 Jonathan died. Martha flew to Middletown for the funeral but was very withdrawn and uncommunicative. Sarah was so devastated by her own loss she wasn't able to see Martha's pain. Martha returned to Billings for a short time but immediately accepted a job in New York. Sarah asked about Greyson and Martha simply said, "That didn't work out." Sarah attempted to learn more, but Martha closed down and offered no more explanation.

For the next fifteen years, Martha and her mother shared hurried conversations on the phone. Her daughter was totally immersed in her work; "I've got to return to the lab, Mom. Sorry," she said so often when Sarah called.

Martha visited Middletown once and returned a second time when her brother's son was killed in an automobile accident.

It came as a tremendous surprise to Sarah when Martha called a couple of years ago to say her firm was opening a branch in Middletown. Martha would be returning to manage the grants and perform research for pharmaceutical companies in the Midwest. As it turned out, Martha had been instrumental in determining that Middletown would be the location of this new branch. *Does she want to reconnect with her family?* Sarah wondered at the time.

Martha had been home now for over two years, and there hadn't been much in the way of reconnecting. One of Martha's few family-oriented activities was to convince Sarah to move out of the family home and into Cunningham Village. Sarah had been very reluctant to move into a retirement community and fought Martha but, in the end, she moved and never regretted it! Martha visited a time or two, met Charles, and visited with her brother and his new wife a few times. And yet, she remained emotionally removed from the family.

When Sarah thought of asking her to come into the shop to help her, she had an ulterior motive. She hoped to reach out to her daughter and begin to build that relationship she felt they both needed.

The two women continued to sit at Sarah's kitchen table without speaking. Finally, Martha raised her head and simply said, "I know we need to talk, Mom. I have so much to explain to you." Tears again welled up in her eyes. "I just can't do it now. If I promise to tell you the whole story soon, will you be patient with me just a little longer?" She looked at her mother pleadingly with both pain and hope in her eyes. For the first time in years, Sarah saw behind the mask.

"Of course, I can be patient. I love you," her mother said with a smile. She stood and walked behind her daughter's chair and kissed her gently on the cheek. Martha began to sob softly and hurried into the guest room, gently closing the door behind her. Sarah began preparing dinner while feeling hopeful about their relationship for the first time in many years.

Martha left around ten and drove home slowly, thinking about the day and wondering if she could ever explain why she had created distance between herself and her family. *When did it start?* she wondered. The face of Greyson materialized in her mind. *Greyson*, she thought. *That's when it all began.*

She loved Greyson from the day they met. She had set all her own hopes and aspirations aside to be with him and follow his dream. He spoke of Montana and nature and family and created a picture of their life together which was enticing. He described the mountains and the snow piled high around a cozy log cabin complete with a roaring fire. He planned to write, and he would talk about the children they would have. His words seduced her into an illusion that took the place of reality.

Unfortunately, her illusion collapsed when she allowed herself to see the real Greyson. She felt trapped and frightened. And then it got worse.

Chapter 6

It was Friday night and the group of ten or so women was sitting around the table in the workroom. "This is our third meeting without Ruth. When do you think your sister will be back with us?" Christina asked, looking toward Anna.

"Sarah has spoken with her more recently than I have. Sarah?" Anna said turning the question over to her.

"I think it could be another month," Sarah responded. "Her mother has rallied somewhat since Ruth's been there."

Kimberly spoke up saying, "Even though this must be a very sad time for her, it's really special that Ruth can spend some time with her mother and in her childhood home."

"It is," Sarah responded as she hemmed her Sunbonnet Sue baby quilt. She started the quilt for Jason and Jennifer's baby, and it was beginning to look as if she would have it finished in time. "She's also getting to know her brother, Jacob. He was a toddler when Ruth left home."

Anna stopped knitting for a moment and looked up. "My sister missed our family for all those years when Papa wouldn't let her visit. It broke Mama's heart, but she never defied him. I'm just glad she is willing to allow Ruth to be there now. It's probably pretty crowded though," she added as she resumed working on the sweater she was knitting for her little Annabelle. "Rebecca and Jacob have two little girls and another on the way."

Allison, looking a little confused, said, "I thought the Amish have a separate house for their grandparents." Allison was new to the group. She was in her early twenties but had been quilting since she was young. She did primarily appliqué and was working on a Baltimore Album quilt as she talked.

"They do," Anna responded, "and we have one as well. It's called a *dawdyhaus*, and it's built just behind the main house. When Jacob and Rebecca were first married, my folks moved into the *dawdyhaus*, but after Mama had her stroke and Papa died, Jacob moved Mama back into her old room."

"Well, tell her we're all praying for her and your mother," Christina responded. "Do you think there's anything we can do for Ruth?"

"I'm glad you brought that up, Christina," Anna responded. "I've been wondering if we could make a quilt for her in honor of our mother."

"What an excellent idea!" Sarah cried. "With all of us working on it, we could probably finish it before Ruth returns. Oh, wait ..." turning to Anna and interrupting herself she added, "I'm sorry, Anna. She's your mother too...." Sarah felt awkward and didn't know how to finish the sentence.

"Mama and I were able to see each other after Papa died and, because I was living in the next community, I was able to visit with the rest of the family even before that. Ruth's the one that went for years with no family connections, and she's the one helping our mother leave this world. A quilt would be very special to her. I was even wondering if we could make something using Amish colors, something that would truly remind Ruth of her home and her family."

"Oh, wonderful!" Sarah exclaimed. "Would you help us design it?"

"I'd be happy to," Anna responded with a joyful smile.

While the others worked on their projects and talked, Anna slipped into the shop and pulled two pattern books off the shelf, both featuring Amish quilts. She looked for ones with repetitive blocks that would be easy for her friends to make at home.

Going back into the workroom later, she showed the group a picture of a nine-patch quilt made with the Amish solids that were popular in her community.

"Don't they use prints?"

"No, just solid colors," Anna responded. "Each community has its own rules about color, but in our community, as long as we use solids and include black, we can use pastels and even bright, vibrant colors in our quilts."

"Why black?" Kimberly asked curiously.

"Black is seen as an emblem of the plain and simple life. You'll see Amish men and women dressed in black, but many Amish communities are more liberal and allow color in women's blouses and men's shirts."

"Amish quilts don't seem very 'plain and simple' to me!" Allison commented.

"But they're warm, and it's a 'plain and simple' truth that homes need blankets, especially homes without electricity!" Anna said with a smile. "Actually," she added with a chuckle, "we Amish women keep it to ourselves that we really *love* getting together for our quilting bees!" Everyone laughed with her, acknowledging the age-old truth that women know how to get around the most oppressive of rules.

"Let's go pick out our colors and," Anna said turning to Sarah, "would it be okay if we go ahead and cut our two-inch strips directly from the bolts so we can start making our nine-patches right away?"

"Sure," Sarah responded. "There's money in the kitty for things like this. Start cutting!" She knew she was going to pick up the bill herself with her inheritance from her Aunt Rose. It wouldn't be right for the fabric to come out of Ruth's profit!

"Everyone pick out two fabrics for your nine patches," Anna called above the confusion and watched as the quilters picked up solid bolts, comparing them in sets of two. "I'll cut you each enough to make some nine-patch blocks this week. Next week we'll see how many we have and, if we need more, we can make them at the next meeting. If you have solids at home and want to make more, go ahead."

"I think I'll do mine in black and purple. I love that combination," Christina said.

"I can take some black too. I'll use mine with green," Sarah asked.

"Should I get black too?" a woman called from across the room.

"I think that's probably enough black for now. We'll use a black border, and if it looks like we need more black in our blocks, we'll add it next week. Sarah, could you cover the cutting table for a few minutes?"

"Sure," Sarah responded taking Anna's place and picking up the rotary cutter. Anna ran to the back room and quickly sketched out the instructions for the block and made copies. She returned to the main room and passed out the instructions, although most of the members already knew how to make a simple two-color nine-patch. "Make as many as you can with the fabric you have and we'll see how many more we need at our next meeting."

Anna was excited about the project. Her sister was going to love the quilt, and she would understand what it meant to her friends to be able to give her this gift from their hands and their hearts.

It was nearly 9:00 p.m. as Charles drove by the shop slowly, trying to see what was going on without being seen. He didn't want Sarah to know he was checking on her safety. Looking toward the front window, he at first thought something was wrong. Women were milling around in what appeared to be a state of confusion. Before he began to panic, however, he noticed they were all carrying bolts of fabric and seemed to be lining up at what he knew was the cutting table.

Poor Sarah, he chuckled to himself, wishing he could go in and help. Instead, he parked up the street waiting for the lights to go off in the shop and for Sarah to be safely in her car heading home.

* * * * *

Saturday morning Martha met Sarah as she was unlocking the door to the shop. "Well, you're sure here early," Sarah said with a smile. "I didn't expect you until this afternoon."

"I thought I should come in early in case the weather gets bad later." Martha took off her coat and boots and carried them to the back room in her sock feet. She sat down and removed her indoor shoes from her tote bag. Sarah kept an extra pair of shoes at the shop, and she also traded her boots for her shop slippers.

It had started snowing around ten the previous night. Sarah had just arrived home when she turned to take Barney out and was surprised to see the large flakes slowly floating to the ground. There was no more than an inch on the ground that morning when she left the house, but the sky was gray and more snow was in the forecast.

"Where's Barney," Martha asked suddenly realizing Sarah had arrived alone.

"I didn't want him tracking snow in and out and leaving puddles that might cause someone to fall. He'll enjoy a day at home on his own. I'll ask Caitlyn to run down this afternoon and take him for a walk."

Caitlyn was Andy's fifteen-year-old daughter and lived with him up the street from Sarah. Residents were required to be over fifty-five, but this was a special circumstance. Caitlyn had come to live with her father after losing her mother and her stepfather. She and Andy had never met, and their year together had been one of getting to know one another. Andy was a kind, gentle man and Caitlyn a very bright, competent young woman, and that made the transition an easy one for both of them. When the management balked about having a youngster in the community, the two were able to convince them that she was there as her elderly father's caregiver. Actually, Andy was one of the youngest residents in the community; but he was well liked by everyone, and the management decided to look the other way.

Caitlyn had become like a granddaughter to Sarah and had been learning to quilt under Sarah's competent tutelage. "I think I'm also going to invite Caitlyn to the Friday Night Quilters," Sarah said. "I think she would fit in nicely. She's very interested in quilting and seems to have a knack for it. We have a young woman in the group that's actually only a few years older than Caitlyn." Sarah was thinking about Allison who was in her early twenties. Of course, those few years can make a big difference. Caitlyn was still in high school, but she had a difficult life before she came to live with Andy and was mature for her age.

"I would like to meet more of your friends," Martha commented, surprising Sarah.

Turning to look at her, Sarah responded, "I would love that, Martha. Maybe we should plan a holiday party after Ruth gets back." Martha heard the gentleness in her mother's voice and felt her love. She wanted to feel excited about planning a party but could feel her past standing in the way.

"I'll talk to Mama tomorrow," Martha said aloud as she drove home. She knew that her mother deserved to know why she had excluded the family from her life.

As she pulled up to the curb, a black car drove slowly past her. It was too dark to see who was driving. She thought for a moment that the driver intended to stop, but suddenly it sped away. *What's that all about?* she wondered.

Chapter 7

"Hi, Mama. Are you free to talk?" Martha stood shivering at Sarah's door early on Sunday morning. Her nose was red and her eyes bloodshot. She had obviously been crying. Sarah put her arms around her daughter, drawing her into the warmth of the house and quickly closing the door. It was a dark, gray morning with a breathtaking chill in the air. She guided Martha into the kitchen where she poured a cup of hot coffee and added cream and sugar the way Martha liked it. Together they sat down at the table, but Martha kept her coat on. "I need it, Mama. I'm freezing."

Twice she called me "Mama," Sarah thought. She hadn't heard Martha use that word for many years. Sarah had become the more formal "mother" when Martha addressed her. Sarah sat quietly giving Martha time to organize her thoughts.

"I promised to explain what's been going on with me over the last twenty years and why I've avoided the family all that time. I know there's no excuse for my behavior, but I want to try to explain my side and maybe you can forgive me."

"Martha, I love you and there's nothing to forgive. You have the right to lead your life anyway you want. ..."

"No, Mama. This isn't the way I want to live my life. It's the way I mistakenly thought I had to live it. Let me try to explain." Again, Martha sat quietly and finally spoke, very softly at first. Sarah had to move in closer to hear her.

"You never asked anything about my marriage to Greyson, but I think you sensed there were problems. I've been so ashamed of bringing him into our family and our lives. I've kept my distance from the family, at first because that's what he wanted. Later it was because I was embarrassed. Then it was to protect you and Jason."

"What do you mean?" Sarah asked, confused by what she was hearing.

Martha's voice was monotone as she recounted the months following their whirlwind marriage. "We headed for Montana and arrived in Billings with no place to stay. His friends were unable to help us. In fact, they were barely functioning themselves."

"What about his family?" Sarah asked.

"The family he told me about was nonexistent. He lied about that. And he lied about going to graduate school. He had never even been to Seattle!"

"For a while, we slept on the couch in a dirty one-bedroom apartment that belonged to one of his disgusting friends. There were others who came and went. It was horrible. I wanted to leave."

Martha lowered her head, looking embarrassed. She hoped her mother didn't ask why she didn't leave. She didn't know what kept her there. *Love, I guess*, she thought. *Misplaced, childish love.* Martha was only twenty-four at the time, and in retrospect, she realized she was a naive child. Martha had graduated high school at sixteen and spent the next eight years working toward her advanced degrees. She had little exposure to the real world. She was a serious student, and by the age of twenty-four, she had spent most of her life in books. *I thought I was so grown-up*, she told herself, *but I wasn't.*

After a while, Martha continued, still in a monotone with tears standing in her eyes. "At first, it wasn't clear how these people were making a living, but after a few weeks it became obvious. They were all involved with drugs: taking them, selling them, and traveling into Mexico to purchase them. At first, I was confused about why Greyson was involved in this world. Why were these people his friends?" Continuing, Martha added, "I threatened to leave him, and he became very angry. Violent, actually."

"Did he hurt you …?" Sarah asked, drawing herself up protectively.

"Sometimes, but he always apologized and pleaded with me to stay. He promised to get a job and find us a place to live. I agreed to have money wired from my account in California to get us established." Lowering her head with embarrassment, she added, "I did that more than once. I did that until my account was empty." She covered her face with her hands and shook her head as if she couldn't believe she had made so many mistakes.

"Finally I got a job with a research firm in Billings and things seemed to be looking up. We rented a small cottage in an older neighborhood in the suburbs. Greyson spent his days looking for work, or at least that's what he said he was doing."

Martha stopped talking and looked at her mother. "Should I continue? Do you want to hear it all?"

"I want to hear the whole story, Martha. The whole story." Sarah stood and refilled their cups and took a few oatmeal cookies out of the cookie jar. They sipped their coffee, but the cookies lay untouched.

Martha went on to explain that a few months later, she inadvertently discovered drugs hidden in the basement of their cottage. Continuing to search, she found large sums of money bundled and hidden in the crawl space behind the furnace. "I was shocked and, at first, I couldn't believe it was Greyson. I wanted to believe someone had left the money and the drugs there. But I knew better. I secretly took our meager savings and hired a private detective."

"You did?" Sarah responded, impressed with her daughter's ingenuity. "You were a brave young woman!"

"He brought me evidence of activities far worse than I had imagined. Greyson was selling drugs at all three high schools and was making overtures to students in two of the four middle schools!"

As Martha talked about the young students and about Greyson, her cheeks grew flushed with anger. She continued talking, and Sarah sat silently in shock and disbelief that her daughter could have gone through all this alone. She wondered why Martha hadn't turned to her family, but she didn't want to interrupt in any way. She hoped that telling the entire story would help Martha purge this nightmare from her life.

Martha continued talking but now with more animation in her voice. She told Sarah about contacting the police and reporting everything she knew. She gave them names and her private detective's report. "I saw an attorney who told me that I couldn't be forced to testify against him, and I was glad. I was afraid of what he might do."

The police assured her they had sufficient evidence without her involvement. "It was at that point that I packed one suitcase and left town, leaving everything behind."

"Where did you go," Sarah asked, wondering why she hadn't come home.

"I went to New York where a friend had promised to get me an interview with a research company. That's the company I'm still with today," she added.

Sarah couldn't hold her tongue another minute. "Why didn't you come home, Martha? I don't understand that part. You know we would have been here for you."

"I know, Mother. He threatened me, and he threatened you and Jason as well. He swore he would kill us all. My attorney said he was making idle threats, but he knew I turned him in and he was blind with anger. When Jason's son was killed. ..." Martha began to sob.

"You think that wasn't an accident?" Sarah cried. "Oh, Martha ..." She placed her hand on her heart and stared at Martha in shock.

"No, Mama. No! We don't know that it was Greyson. It was probably an accident just like the police said. It's just that ..."

"You wondered?" she completed Martha's sentence.

"Yes. I wondered if it were possible. I contacted Greyson after that, and he assured me he had nothing to do with it. He sounded contrite about the drugs and the past, but I didn't know whether to believe him. Nevertheless, to be safe I let him know that you were all out of my life forever. I thought that would keep him away."

"What happened to him?" Sarah asked.

"He was convicted and sent to prison for twenty years. We were all safe from him once he was incarcerated, but I had been so frightened I guess I just couldn't give it up. I continued to think I had to protect us all, and so I stayed as far away from the family as possible."

"He was sentenced to twenty years?" Sarah commented. "That seems like a long time."

"Another one of his little secrets," Martha responded with disgust. "This wasn't his first conviction!"

Sarah had another question that she had to word carefully. "Martha, you've been home for over two years. During that time, it seems like you have continued to be distant from the family. I don't understand that part."

Martha dropped her eyes. "I was ashamed, Mama. I knew I had to explain about Greyson, and I was so ashamed. I'm sorry. You know I love you."

"And insisting that I move to Cunningham Village? Was that because of Greyson too?" Sarah asked, suddenly seeing the connection.

"Yes. I wanted you to be in a protected place with security and friends. You were alone after Daddy died, and you were vulnerable." Smiling, she added, "None of us is in danger anymore. I haven't heard from him for years. He has forgotten all about us.

Martha and Sarah spent the rest of the day together. Once the story was told and the tears shed, the two women decided to bundle up and take a long walk. The snow had stopped and the roads were icy. There was no traffic, and they made their way to the park adjoining Cunningham Village. The limbs were ice covered and the sun was beginning to break through the clouds causing the trees to sparkle as if they were encased in glass.

When they got to the dog park, Sarah removed Barney's leash and headed for a bench. Sarah was surprised to see Martha bend down and scoop up a handful of snow. She carefully formed a snowball while Barney watched with curiosity. She suddenly tossed it at Barney, aiming just behind his back paws. He jumped out of the way, looked at her with surprise and then realized it was a game. He lowered his head and began running in large circles just skimming her boots as he passed behind her. She started chasing him, Martha laughing and Barney barking his excited, playful bark. Tears rose to Sarah's eyes seeing her daughter fighting her way back into the world of the living.

Martha and Sarah spent the rest of the day together and walked over to the Center to meet Charles. After a very pleasant dinner, Charles walked them back to Sarah's house, and they waved as Martha drove away. "I've never seen her so relaxed. She seemed happy tonight," Charles said as they went into the house.

Sarah smiled and responded, "She got a lot off her mind today. I think she's on her way back."

They took their snow covered boots off and sat down on the couch with Barney curled up across their feet. Sarah told Charles what she had learned that afternoon. "I think it has helped her to talk about it." Charles sat quietly letting the facts sink in. Sarah had told the story from a mother's point of view; Charles heard it as a cop. His years in law enforcement had trained him to hear what others missed.

"Your grandson. I remember when that happened."

"Do you think ...?" Sarah began but was still unable to put words on her fear.

"No, Sarah. I don't think so. I talked to the investigators back then. It was an accident." He knew that would reassure her. But he knew it could also have been a warning. *A very cruel warning from a deranged person.*

They continued to sit quietly each deep in private thoughts. He slipped his arm around her and gently pulled her toward him. She laid her head on his chest, feeling the tension that had built up over a very emotion-filled day drain away. He wrapped his other arm around her and held her close letting his warmth and his love offer solace.

Chapter 8

"You wanted me to stop by?" Caitlyn said as she stood at the front door, her teeth chattering.

"Come in quickly," Sarah said pushing the storm door open against the strong winter wind. "I didn't mean for you to weather this storm," she added helping the young girl off with her wraps. "You are freezing!" she said, gently touching Caitlyn's cheek.

"Papa and I went out to shovel snow. We did yours and Sophie's too." Sarah peeked out the front window and saw what they had done. "Oh my! Thank you! I was hoping I wouldn't have to wade through two feet of snow to get to Sophie's house tonight." Looking across the street, she saw that Sophie's walkway was shoveled as well. Cunningham Village management provided snow removal but, with such a heavy snow, she knew it would be a couple of days before they got to the individual walkways. They had been working on the streets and sidewalks since it stopped snowing early that morning.

"Would you like to warm up with a cup of hot cocoa?"

"Yes!" Caitlyn replied joyfully as she saw Barney heading for her at top speed. She met him on the floor just as he reached her, and the two tussled playfully while Sarah hurried into the kitchen. Once they were settled at the table, Sarah explained why she wanted to talk to Caitlyn. She told her about the Friday Night Quilters and the project they were going to be working on for Ruth. "We have a young woman in the group that I think is in her early twenties. Last year we had a young man too. I guess I'm saying this because I want you to know this is not a group of *little ol' ladies*." Caitlyn giggled and Sarah continued. "I was wondering if you might like to come to one or two meetings just to see if you might like it."

Caitlyn's cheeks flushed with embarrassment as a young girl's often will. "Me?"

"Sure. Why not you? You've had some lessons and even made a quilt for your dad. I think you might enjoy spending time at the shop and getting to know the quilters." They sat quietly sipping their cocoa while Caitlyn mulled over the idea.

"Well, I could come once and just see. Do you think they'll mind?"

"Mind? They'll be delighted. Besides, Barney would love having you there."

"Barney?" Caitlyn exclaimed with surprise. "Barney goes?"

"Sure. Barney goes every Friday night. He's an honorary member." It was clear to Sarah that Barney's presence at the club made all the difference.

"I'll go," she responded eagerly. "It sounds like fun."

"Okay, then I want to show you our project and see if you will help me with it. Are you free for an hour or so?"

"Sure. Papa went on up the street to dig out a couple of older folks in the next block. Mr. Dumfries' been sick and

Papa wanted to get there before the old guy tries to do it himself." She smiled with pride.

"Okay then. Let's head for the sewing room." Sarah pulled out the strips she brought for Ruth's quilt and the instructions for making a nine-patch. She told Caitlyn to read the directions while she got their supplies set up. Together they laid out the strips, and Caitlyn sat down at the machine. As she sewed the strips together, she passed them to Sarah for pressing. As soon as they had them sewn into groups of three, Sarah showed the young girl how to cut them and pin them together to form the nine-patches. Sarah took over at the machine and did the final stitching, while Caitlyn pressed the finished blocks. Within an hour, they had completed twenty green and black quilt blocks ready to be added to Ruth's quilt.

"But these are yours. Can I make some of my own for her quilt?" Caitlyn asked as they were making plans for taking the nine-patch blocks to the next meeting.

"Sure you may," Sarah responding feeling proud of her young protégé. "I'll bring home another set of strips, and you can do them by yourself if you would like. What colors do you want?" While they were working, Sarah had told her about the color restrictions of the Amish community.

"Could I use pink?" Without waiting for a response, Caitlyn added eagerly, "How about pink and yellow? Would that look okay?"

"That would be very striking, and the yellow will add that important *sparkle* to the quilt! I'll bring the strips home tomorrow, and you let me know when you can come over."

"I can come anytime. Maybe tomorrow after you get home?"

"What about your homework?" Sarah asked, not wanting to interfere with her studies.

"Snow, remember? School is closed for a few days." Caitlyn looked ecstatic about being out of school even though she loved it and was an excellent student according to her father who was just a bit biased.

Sarah and Barney walked Caitlyn to the door and Barney tried to slip out with her. "Barney, stay!" Sarah commanded gently.

"Could I take him for a little walk?" Caitlyn pleaded holding on to him by his collar.

Sarah laughed and said, "Sure. I'll get his leash." As the two walked away, Sarah was choked up with emotion. She had grown to love this very brave, independent young woman.

* * * * *

"What took you so long," Sophie demanded as Sarah stomped the snow off her boots before stepping inside.

"Have you looked outside?" Sarah retorted. It had started snowing again, and both walkways were covered. Sophie had invited Sarah to come have an early dinner with her and to share some news which she refused to discuss on the phone. Sophie had cheese and crackers ready, along with a chilled bottle of Chardonnay. Once they got comfortable in the living room in front of Sophie's new electric fireplace, Sarah could wait no longer.

"Okay, Sophie. Give. What's this news you are teasing me with?"

"Timothy is coming." Sophie beamed with happiness. Sophie's son was in his fifties and had moved to Alaska right after graduating from high school. All through high school, he had followed the progress of the Alaska pipeline and dreamed of being involved.

At seventeen, he packed his boots and parka and drove to Anchorage. For the next thirty years, he worked along the 800-mile pipeline. He didn't have a degree but learned engineering on the job.

"How does he stand the cold?"

"I guess you get used to it. He never mentions it. Anyway, he'll be here next week, and he's staying for two months! I can hardly wait!" Sarah had never seen Sophie so excited.

"I'm hoping he might decide to stay," Sophie added. "Occasionally he writes about retiring. I wish he would. He's in his fifties, and he's been doing hard physical work for many years."

"Well, he's still young," Sarah responded. *When did I start thinking of fifty as young*, she wondered.

The two had dinner in Sophie's kitchen while Sophie told tales of Timothy's exploits in Alaska. She read Sarah two of his letters written in the mid-1980s describing the hardships at that time. "He'd only been there a couple of years and was very young. He never questioned his decision, though. This work was his life's dream!"

Around 8:00, Sarah announced that she should be trudging on home. "… before our street looks like Alaska!" she added. The snow had started up again, and the path Andy had dug for them was no longer visible. "Looks like Andy has his work cut out for tomorrow," she chuckled as she carefully picked her way across the street.

Not wanting to go back out, she opened the kitchen door and pushed a reluctant Barney outside for his final outing of the day. Watching him plow his way through the deep snow, she thought about Timothy Ward and wondered what his life had been like. She was glad she would have a chance to hear about it.

Chapter 9

"Remember that serious talk we were going to have?" Sarah and Charles were sitting at the Bedford Lodge outside of town. The waitress had seated them by the window, looking out over the rolling fields covered with glistening white snow. The boughs of fir trees in the distance were weighted down. The snow drifted against the outbuildings and fences. It was barely dusk, and the waitress lit the candle on their table. Simultaneously, someone switched on the outdoor spotlights, giving the grounds a dreamlike appearance.

"Yes, I remember," Sarah said dropping her eyes.

Does that look mean she doesn't want to talk about it? Has she changed her mind? Or is she simply looking coy? Charles sighed. He found it exasperating to try to interpret all the many looks this lovely woman had at her disposal. He had never been good at the subtle, unless of course, it was the subtleness of a criminal attempting to look innocent. *That* he could interpret immediately. He had to admit, however, that it was always the male criminal he was able to read. Not the females. He had a partner who handled the women. Charles had been married for many years to the same woman and, until the day she died, she said what she meant and was *never* subtle.

Sarah looked up and responded saying, "I guess we need to talk, Charles. I know there are things you want to say. I'm just …"

"Hesitant?" he suggested after a short pause.

"Hesitant? Yes, I guess that's the word. Maybe. It's just that I've been so happy the way things are. I haven't been this happy for years. I guess I'm worried about ruining that."

"Do you think marriage would ruin that?"

"*Marriage!?*" she almost choked on her drink, then looked around to see if anyone had noticed. Lowering her voice, she responded, "I didn't know we were talking about *marriage*. I must admit that I thought you were talking about …" she paused.

"Sex?" he suggested, again helping her get the words out. She looked around again, hoping no one was paying attention.

"Look Sarah," Charles continued. "I'm an old-fashioned guy. I know it's not popular these days, but I just believe in certain things, and marriage is one of those things."

At first Sarah felt relieved. She still hadn't resolved her feelings about becoming intimate with Charles. *But marriage?* She definitely didn't know how she felt about that. She loved her life and her independence. She loved her little house and being her own woman. She loved the fact that she never had to explain or account for her actions to someone else. *Or do I just find all those things safe?* she often wondered.

Again, Sarah had a look that Charles didn't understand. *Is she upset by the thought of marriage? Confused? Totally against the idea?* Charles knew he had to stop second-guessing and simply ask. It frightened him to do it since he would have to accept her response even it was not what he wanted to hear.

"What are you thinking, Sarah?"

Sarah remained quiet for a long moment, and then began talking. She told him about her devastation when her husband died suddenly and the months of rebuilding her life. She told him about returning to her job and later moving to the retirement village. She talked about living on her own for the first time and how she had learned to enjoy her freedom and independence.

"Marriage scares you," he responded simply.

"Yes, it scares me."

"It scares me too," he responded, "but life without you scares me even more."

They both sat quietly looking into each other's eyes. The waitress had left menus earlier but, noticing that they laid untouched, she hadn't interrupted the couple again. Sarah's mind went to their last night on the cruise as they stood looking at the moon while the ship sliced its way through the dark waters. She remembered the warmth of his arms and the desire.

Charles interrupted her thoughts saying, "Sarah, I want you to be my wife. I don't want to rush you, and I certainly don't want to lose you. If marriage isn't what you want, we'll work it out."

"I love you, Charles," she said simply. Tears were standing in both their eyes. He reached across the table and gently touched her cheek.

"To be continued," he said gently with a loving smile as he picked up his menu.

* * * * *

It was three days after their dinner at the Bedford Lodge, and Sarah's head was still spinning. She hadn't told anyone about their conversation but had decided to talk about it with Martha. She thought Martha might understand her reservations, although she had to admit that she didn't understand it herself. Charles was a good man, a gentle and kind man, and he loved her.

"And do you love him?" Martha asked.

"Of course, I do, but it's a comfortable love, not the kind you see in the movies. And the idea of being a seventy-year-old bride concerns me," she told Martha.

"Why is that?" Martha asked, looking confused. "You would make a beautiful bride." Martha was beginning to think that her mother was coming up with excuses to avoid marrying Charles. "What's really bothering you, Mama?"

"I don't want to give up my independence," she responded, looking away.

"Well, mother, I guess this is something only you can answer. He's a good man. My brother and I think he's good for you and an incredible addition to our family; in fact, Jason said it would be great to have another man in the family!" In a more serious tone, she continued, "but only you can decide if you want to be married. I know what you're saying about your independence. I've been alone as long as you have and I'm sure it would be hard for me to allow someone into my life."

"You understand what I'm dealing with here," Sarah said, glad to finally be heard. Sophie had been telling her she was crazy.

Martha continued, "But I think there is a middle ground that a couple can find. We should be able to be as independent as we wish and yet enjoy the comfort of having someone to depend on when we need it."

"The other side of that coin, I suppose," Sarah said thoughtfully, "is that the other person would be depending on us some of the time as well."

"Yes," Martha responded. "The give and take of a good relationship! That's what it's all about."

Sarah mulled this over for a while as she and Martha restacked the fat quarters into their appropriate bins and returned bolts of fabric to the shelves. "Maybe my concern is not just the concept of my independence, but maybe what I fear would happen with Charles."

"What's that?" Martha asked, stopping to give her mother her full attention.

"As an ex-cop, he's accustomed to always being on the lookout for danger. I'm constantly reminding him to step back and let me take care of myself. Sometimes he makes me feel like a child who needs adult supervision!"

Martha laughed. "How did you get to be such a liberated woman?"

"Is that liberated? It just feels like common sense."

"Charles is an old-fashioned kind of guy, Mother. He opens doors for you and picks up the check on your dates. He likes to think he is doing the manly thing. I don't think that means he would take away your independence or ever treat you like a child. He clearly respects and loves you for the woman you are. I just think he's in his seventies and sees his role from that perspective."

"Hmm," Sarah responded sounding rather noncommittal.

"Also," Martha added, "as a cop, it's second nature for him to be watchful."

"There's something I haven't told you," Sarah began in a lowered conspiratory voice. "The first night that I stayed at Stitches during the evening, he was lurking up the street."

"Lurking?" Martha responded with surprise.

"Well, he was parked up the street watching until I got into my car."

"Then what did he do?" Martha asked with mounting concern.

"Went home, I guess. I don't know."

Martha suddenly realized what Charles had been doing. She laughed and said, "Mother! *Lurking?* He was just looking out for you. He didn't take away a bit of your independence. But if there had been a problem, he would have been there to help you. I think that's sweet."

"How did you get to be such an old-fashioned girl?" They both laughed, and Sarah gave her daughter a hug.

"We'll figure this out together, Mama, I promise."

Chapter 10

Sarah was finishing her fourth week at Stitches and was feeling very comfortable with her new role. A new quilter had come into the shop that morning feeling overwhelmed by her project and asking if she could return her unused supplies. She was ready to give up quilting.

Sarah took her into the classroom and gave her a cup of tea. The woman introduced herself as Cindy and said she was just too frustrated to make sense of the instructions. Sarah looked over the project, and within an hour she had sorted out the problem and demonstrated the steps Cindy needed to take in order to complete one block.

Cindy felt comfortable with that and asked about the next step after the blocks were finished. Sarah suggested she bring her blocks into the shop, and she would help her put them together and add borders.

"Borders?" the woman exclaimed. "I forgot about borders. Should I buy those now?"

"Let's wait until we get the blocks together, and then we can walk through the shop and audition possible border fabrics."

"Audition?" Cindy repeated. "I like that!" Before she left the shop, Cindy asked about classes and Sarah recommended one of the beginning classes Ruth would be offering in the spring.

On her way out the door, Cindy turned and said "I would love to make that wall quilt hanging behind the cash register. It would look really nice in my house."

Cindy had entered the shop looking discouraged and ready to give up quilting. She left the shop excitedly talking about her next project. *A new customer for Ruth!* Sarah thought with a smile. *I can do this!*

"And did you enjoy teaching?" Ruth asked when she called later that day.

"Yes! I loved it. I think I would like to design a beginning class. Would that be okay? You don't have to pay me. I just think it would be fun."

Ruth laughed and said, "Oh, you'll get paid. We'll charge the students, and you can have whatever they pay. They'll be buying their fabric from me, so we'll both be winners!"

They continued to talk about the shop and about Ruth's mother. The previous week Ruth had felt her mother was rallying, but this week she had been in and out of consciousness. "Or maybe she is just sleeping, we can't really tell. At least she's peaceful," Ruth had said. "How's the Friday night club coming along? Do you have a project?"

Sarah was caught off-guard with the question and stumbled somewhat with her answer. "Well, Anna's handling all that," she said desperately searching for the right words. "Oh! I wanted to tell you," quickly changing the subject, "Caitlyn is coming this week. She has agreed to give the club a try. I know she's young, but ..."

"Never too young!" Ruth interjected. "I'm so glad. Bring Barney along too just in case she gets bored." After they hung up, Sarah straightened up the shop and locked the door.

Two hours later, she was back and unlocking the door. Caitlyn and Barney were eager to get in out of the cold. Just then Kimberly pulled up to the curb and hopped out of her car. "Where's Christina?" Sarah called to her as she approached the door.

"The technician who services our long-arm machine is at the house. She sent her blocks with me, and she's hoping to get here later."

As the group pulled the tables together to make one large work area, they pulled out their squares. Anna had made twenty blocks and had sewn them together so the group could see what the quilt was going to look like. She held it up and the group expressed their approval.

"Oh …"

"Beautiful!"

"I love it!"

They put all their blocks on the table and organized them by color. "I think we need about fifty more blocks," Anna said. "What colors do we need more of?"

"If we want to accent black, I think we need more blocks with black. Maybe black with purple or maybe with blue," Delores volunteered. Delores had taken classes the previous year with her granddaughter, Danielle. Later she had joined the Friday Night Quilters, but Danielle, now fifteen, wasn't interested. Sarah looked at Delores and wondered if Danny might be willing to come now that Caitlyn was coming.

She made a mental note to discuss it with Delores after the meeting.

Caitlyn proudly placed her fifteen blocks on the table and the group praised her work, causing her to blush. Sarah smiled like a proud grandmother. The group decided to make the additional blocks during the meeting. They set up two sewing machines and two ironing boards and started cutting strips. The strips were passed to Kimberly for pinning and on to one of the sewers. Sarah took up her post at one of the ironing boards, and Anna ran around overseeing the project.

Within an hour, they had finished and were ready to put the blocks together in rows. With everyone working, they pinned, sewed, and pressed until the top was finished. "It's almost 10:30, girls," Anna called. "Let's clean up." By 11:00, they were ready to leave. Their meeting had run an extra two hours, but no one seemed to mind. They were excited about having completed the quilt top so quickly.

"I'll take it home and put the borders on, okay?" Anna suggested.

"Do we need to pick out border fabric?" someone called out.

"No. It really should be black in order to be traditional. I'm thinking about doing a thin black border first, then a slightly wider turquoise border, and finish with a wider black."

"Striking!" Sarah responded. "Are we going to hand quilt it?"

"Let's not be *that* traditional," Kimberly called out. "I would be happy to quilt it on my long-arm machine."

Everyone agreed, and they headed for the door chattering excitedly.

"Wait!" Kimberly called out suddenly. "Anna, what would you think about having the group meet at my house next week? We could go through the patterns and chose a quilting pattern, and we could even get the quilt on the machine, and I could run a couple of rows so everyone could see the machine in action."

"Fantastic idea! What do you think folks?" Everyone agreed, and Kimberly promised to email directions to her house the next day.

"Well, Caitlyn, how did you like that?" Sarah asked as they were driving home.

"I loved it! Can I come next week too?"

"You sure may, young lady," Sarah responded with a loving smile. "You sure may."

Chapter 11

Martha continued to enjoy having Alan Fitzgerald in her department. He was an excellent employee, requiring little or no supervision and had taken much of the routine burden from her shoulders, enabling her to concentrate on her own management issues. She was in the process of reorganizing the department and was meeting with Alan daily to discuss the various functions and identify staff for each unit. She had decided to promote Alan to a management position overseeing the new units. She knew he could handle the responsibility, and it would enable her to concentrate on her own research and to pursue new contracts.

Martha tried not to notice how attractive Alan was but found it difficult. His subtle cologne wafted past her many times a day as he walked by her desk en route to the lab. She wondered about his wife and wished she had married a man like Alan instead of Greyson. But then, Greyson had fooled her into thinking he was someone else. She thought about her mother's hesitation about making a commitment to Charles and could understand how hard it must be for her to consider changing the very comfortable life she had created for herself. *It's all so hard*, she told herself as she turned to her microscope, appreciating the predictability of her work.

Leaving early that night, she stopped at a local sandwich shop where she picked up the "to go" order she had placed before leaving the office. As she approached her house, a car was just pulling away from the curb. She wasn't expecting anyone and figured they were visiting one of her neighbors.

As Martha walked toward her front door, she noticed an envelope sticking behind her mailbox. She grabbed the envelope and then reached inside the box to remove the other mail. Laying the envelope and the mail on the table in the foyer, she removed her boots and placed them aside to dry. As she was hanging up her coat, she began to wonder why the envelope wasn't in the box with the other mail. She picked it up again, and this time with mild trepidation, noticing that it was not addressed nor stamped. Opening it, she found a handwritten letter. She quickly dropped down to the signature and was surprised to see that it was from Derek Kettler, the employee she had fired.

Martha went into the living room, turned on the light, and sat down to read the one-page letter. She quickly scanned the entire letter, then went back to read it more carefully. The letter left her feeling confused. *Why did he write this?*

Dear Martha,

I'm sorry it took me so long to contact you. I don't know what got into me the night we had dinner. I abruptly tried to kiss you, and that must have been very upsetting for you. I deserved the slap you gave me.

I know I performed disgracefully on the job, as well, and I completely understand why you had to let me go. I just hoped then, and continue to hope now, that we can continue to be friends and give ourselves the opportunity to find out if there could be more. Please don't discount the possibilities.

Derek

Martha sat holding the letter and trying to make sense of it. *Continue to be friends? Don't discount the possibilities?* "What possibilities?" she said aloud. "This man is totally out of touch with reality."

Martha folded the letter and placed it in a desk drawer. She wondered briefly if she'd done anything to encourage him or to make him think they were friends. She felt certain she hadn't given him the wrong message since she had made every attempt to avoid him at the office. *But then I did go to dinner with him. I shouldn't have done that*, she realized. *But how could I have known?*

She didn't know how to respond to the letter, but decided it really didn't require a response. She reached into the desk, removed the letter, and dropped it in the trash can.

* * * * *

As she was warming up her lasagna, the phone rang three times, but by the time she answered there was no one on the line.

The missed-call feature simply read "private caller."

Chapter 12

Timothy Ward was scheduled to arrive on a Friday afternoon, and Sophie had a party planned for the next day to introduce him to her friends. Once the guest list got beyond thirty, Sophie decided to rent space in the community center.

"I would like to bring Martha if that's okay with you," Sarah asked.

"Of course! She's already on the guest list!" Sophie responded.

"Is Barney on the guest list?" she asked in a teasing tone.

"Do you think I want my son exposed to that flea-bitten mutt?" Sophie responded, slipping a piece of her sandwich under the table to Barney.

"No table scraps, Sophie! You know better."

"How do you think dogs survived for generations before canned Mutt Morsels was invented?"

"Still, no table scraps."

"Okay, okay. Sorry pal," she said patting Barney's head under the table and slipping the last of her potato chips into his eager mouth.

When Sarah got home from Stitches the next day, Sophie came hobbling out of her house at a disturbing speed, considering the sidewalk was icy.

"Slow down, Sophie! I'll come over there." Sarah hurried across the street to see what had her friend in such a tizzy only to discover that Timothy had arrived, and Sophie was eager for her friend to meet him.

"This is my son, Timothy," Sophie said proudly as Timothy appeared at the door. They exchanged the usual polite greetings, and Timothy asked her to come in. Sarah was taken aback by his appearance. She hadn't expected him to be such a big man. He was well over six feet tall and towered over his mother. He was broad shouldered and apparently in excellent shape. I guess *that's what a lifetime of physical work does for you*, she thought. His hair was long, and a full beard covered part of his rugged, deeply tanned face. He had a deep baritone voice and a smile that was infectious.

"I'm eager to meet your dog," he said in his baritone voice. "I understand he's won numerous awards as the ugliest dog in town." It was immediately evident that he shared his mother's brand of humor.

"Okay. I see you *are* your mother's son. Just wait until you meet Barney. He's beautiful, and you'll immediately love him."

"Beautiful like a warthog," Sophie quietly interjected.

Wanting to protect her furry friend, Sarah changed the subject saying, "I'm eager to hear about your work, Timothy."

"Call me Tim, and folks accuse me of not having anything else to talk about but the pipeline, so I'm sure I'll bore you to tears over the next couple of months."

Sophie served coffee and brought out her cookie jar. Sarah was surprised to see her bring the whole jar to the table. She usually spread the cookies out on a plate. "You still have my old cookie jar?" Tim chuckled with surprise as he scooped up a generous handful of his favorite cookies.

After spending a short time with the newly united Ward family, Sarah hurried home to freshen up and get ready for the quilt group meeting.

That evening as Sarah arrived at Kimberley and Christina's house, she was greeted by an enthusiastic group who were all clambering to hear about Sophie's son. "I understand you told Anna he was a hunk!" Christina said laughing. Caitlyn, who had entered with Sarah, blushed probably at the thought of Sarah referring to *anyone* as a hunk.

After Sarah filled the women in on what little she knew about Timothy, the group headed for the back room to see the long-arm quilting machine. The room they were using for the large machine was an addition their father had added for his mother when she began having trouble with the stairs. As they walked through the house, Kimberly explained that her father and her grandfather had built the house from a ready-to-assemble house kit they ordered from the Sears Roebuck catalog in the 1930s. Kimberly and Christina had moved into the house after their parents died.

They were all surprised when they saw the size of the machine. It took up most of the room and left little room for such a large group. The frame and rollers appeared to be about twelve feet long and had an industrial sewing machine attached. Kimberly had already put a quilt on the machine, along with the batting and backing fabric to use as demonstration. She pulled out a stack of patterns and explained how they were used to guide the machine across the fabric.

Caitlyn spoke up saying, "I know this is a silly question, but what does this machine do?"

Kimberly ran the machine down one row and showed Caitlyn how it sewed the pieced top, the batting, and the back together. "It's what people do when they hand quilt. They are just sewing the three layers together. This is just lots faster!"

Caitlyn examined the pattern and then looked through the other patterns Kimberly had laid out. "I like this one," she said holding up an intricate floral pattern.

"That's exactly the one I was going to suggest we use for Ruth's quilt! With all the solid colors, this pattern will add interest." Turning to find Anna, she added, "Anna, is this pattern too fancy?"

Anna laughed. "Now that's where the Amish idea of staying *plain and simple* falls apart. Their quilting is very elaborate. Of course, it's done by hand, but it's the place where the Amish women's artistic skills can be expressed." Walking over to look at the pattern closely, she added, "I love this one, Caitlyn. I think you chose well. Let's do this one if everyone agrees." They passed the pattern around for everyone to see, and they all agreed it was perfect for the quilt. Caitlyn looked pleased.

"What shall we do with the rest of our meeting?" Sarah asked, realizing they had completed their only agenda item.

"I brought hand sewing just in case we had time."

"Me too," Delores added as she looked around but didn't see a place to sit.

"Let's go into the living room," Christina suggested. "I have light snacks in the kitchen and I also thought we would put Ruth's quilt on the machine and get set up for stitching tomorrow. Would anyone like to watch the process?" Since everyone responded with enthusiasm, they decided that two at a time would stay in the room with the two sisters while the others enjoyed the refreshments and worked on their projects.

* * * * *

The next afternoon, Martha drove home smiling as she thought about the success she and her mother had at the shop that day. There'd been a rush of customers in the afternoon, and when she cashed out she discovered that it had been their best Saturday yet. Martha was beginning to look forward to her Saturday's at the shop. She had become proficient at cutting fabric and even offered her opinion on color combinations when asked. She especially loved being there with her mother. Every day she learned things about her that she'd been too young to realize in the past. Her mother was engaged in life, something Martha had never learned to do.

As she turned the corner onto her block, she noticed a black car parked across the street from her house. The car looked familiar, but she couldn't place where she had seen it. As she approached, she could see someone sitting in the driver's seat, but it was dusk and she couldn't make out the person's features. She parked, as usual, in front of her own house and glanced at the car across the street as she was getting out. The driver pulled away from the curb and continued up the street without turning the lights on until reaching the next block. *Curious*, she thought as she hurried into her house and locked the door.

After relaxing in a warm bath, Martha took a cursory look in her closet and thumbed through her pantsuits not sure what to wear to Sophie's party. She didn't know Sophie very well but was glad she was invited to the party, although somewhat surprised. "I won't know anyone," she told her mother earlier that day.

"You know me," her mother had responded. "And you know Sophie and Charles, and you'll recognize some of the women that come into the shop. And you met Andy, didn't you? Caitlyn's dad?"

"Yes, I met Andy briefly. He sounds like a colorful character: a friend, a criminal, a convict, a fugitive, and now a model father."

"And a teacher at the prison. Don't forget that!" Sarah had added. "We all love Andy."

Martha hung the pantsuit she had chosen back in the closet and pulled out a red silk dress she had bought several years before for an office party. She smiled as she slipped it on, pleased that it still fit, but when she looked at herself in the mirror she flashed back to that party and the way Derek had looked at her. "Thank you for wearing such a pretty dress," he had said. At the time, she thought it was a strange thing to say, but in retrospect, she had to wonder if he thought she wore it just for him. The thought sent a shiver up her spine. She started to take the dress off but admonished herself for the thought. *He will not control me!* she told herself firmly, flashing back to the years she had allowed Greyson to control her.

She heard Charles and Sarah pulling up outside her house and, seconds later Charles was ringing the doorbell. "You two didn't need to drive all the way over here to pick me up," she said as she pulled the door closed behind her. "The party is minutes from your house!"

"No problem at all, young lady. We were happy to. I'm going to be the designated driver tonight so you girls can kick up your heels and enjoy the party." Martha again thought about how happy she was that her mother had this kind man in her life.

"Thanks Charles. I'm in the mood for some heel kicking!"

When they arrived at the community center, the music was playing and Sophie was stationed at the entrance decked out in her holiday best and wearing her new large frame purple glasses studded with rhinestones. She had purchased a white sequined pantsuit for the cruise the previous fall, but she had decided to save it for the holidays. With Timothy coming, she decided this was the time to bring it out.

Standing next to Sophie's chair was a striking man with broad shoulders, a full beard, and a deep tan. He had a rugged, manly look that immediately caught Martha's attention.

"Timothy, this is Martha Miller, Sarah's daughter. Martha, my son, Timothy." Martha extended her hand and he took it, surprising her with his gentleness.

"Happy to meet you, *Miss* Miller?" he responded emphasizing the word *Miss* in a questioning tone.

"Yes, it's *Miss*, but call me Martha, please," she replied with a smile.

"Why don't you two help yourselves to drinks and hors d'oeuvres? I'll holler if I have anyone else for you to meet,

Timmy. Actually, I think everyone is here now," Sophie said excitedly, looking around the room. Spotting Sarah, she called out, "Sarah! Come over here with me!"

Sarah walked over looking feminine in her mauve and brown dress. She hoped it wasn't too young for her, but she loved the colors. "It's a wonderful party, Sophie," she said as she approached her glittering friend. About that time, a three-piece country band started playing, and the young man on the guitar began to sing. The guests had been milling around, and they became quiet and moved toward their tables.

Sophie noticed with pleasure that Timothy and Martha had taken seats together. Charles joined them and was looking around for Sarah. When he spotted her, she held up two fingers indicating he should hold two more seats. He understood as he always did, and he tilted their three chairs against the table and walked toward Sarah. "When do we eat?" he asked lightly as he approached.

"How rude!" Sophie responded frowning, but they both knew she was kidding. "Actually, I'm starving too!" she added. "Let's get this show on the road." She signaled one of the caterers who was standing nearby and told him to begin serving.

The evening began to break up around eleven. Most of the guests were in their seventies and weren't accustomed to late hours. Charles was in the process of gathering up his charges when he noticed Timothy bend over and lightly kiss Martha on the cheek as he was saying goodbye. She responded with a smile and a nod and didn't seem to mind. "Interesting," he said aloud.

"What's interesting?" Sarah asked.

"You daughter just got a little peck on the cheek."

"Good!" she responded. "She needs a peck on the cheek!"

As they arrived in front of her house, Martha surreptitiously glanced up and down the block and was pleased to see no extraneous cars. She'd had a good time and was fascinated with this man with so many interesting tales to tell about a part of the country that was foreign to her. He described Alaska as a *barren paradise* and his descriptions peaked her interest.

She smiled as she climbed the stairs to her bedroom. It had been an interesting evening. Timothy Ward had asked if he could call her, and she said yes. She was surprised with herself.

Once she reached her bedroom, she flipped on the light and walked over to the window. As she reached to pull down the shade, she saw a movement in the shadows.

She quickly turned off the light and returned to the window but couldn't see anything.

My imagination is working overtime, she assured herself with a smile. She pulled down the shade, turned on the light, and continued with her evening routine.

Across the street from her house, the glow of a burning cigarette fell to the ground where it burned itself out.

Chapter 13

"**M**om! Pick up! *Mom!*" The man's voice was so distraught Sarah didn't immediately recognize it as her son, Jason. "Call me on my cell. We're at the hospital. It's time!"

Sarah called Charles, knowing he would want to be with her, and he said he would be right over to pick her up. She then called Martha, but there was no answer. She left a message telling her to come over to City Hospital when she got home. Then she called Sophie.

"The baby is here?"

"No, not yet, but Jenny's in the hospital, and Jason said it's time, so we're heading right over."

"Should I come?" Sophie asked hesitantly.

"Why don't you stay here with Timothy. I'll call you as soon as I know something." She then added, "Oh, would you ask Tim to take Barney for a walk in a couple of hours? I'll leave the key under the mat."

"Charles will love that!" Sophie responded sarcastically, knowing how protective he was.

"We won't be telling Charles."

Nevertheless, Charles got a glimpse of the shiny object under the mat and immediately removed it and frowned. "I thought …" he began, but Sarah interrupted him.

"I know what you thought, Charles," Sarah responded impatiently. "You told me not to put the key under the mat, but this is an emergency. Tim needs to use it to take Barney out while we're gone."

"I'll run it over to Sophie," he announced as he hurried across the street without waiting for Sarah's response. Sarah stood frowning in his direction wondering if they would ever be able to find that comfortable compromise between his over protectiveness and her independence.

"It's my key and my house and my decision," she mumbled as she headed for his car. She quickly opened her own door and got in before he could return and open it for her. He stopped when he reached the car and saw that she was already seated inside. He shook his head and got in.

"I get the message," he said as he started the car.

"Good," she responded quietly. But the coolness only lasted for a few blocks as the excitement of a new baby in the family warmed their hearts.

"Do they have a name for her yet?"

"Yes, but they won't tell me. Jenny thinks it's bad luck." Sarah reached down and pulled her island tote onto her lap. "I brought the Sunbonnet Sue quilt for her," she said as she pulled it out and ran her fingers over the delicate appliqués. She had started the quilt on the quilting cruise she had taken earlier that fall, and she had completed it just in time for the baby's arrival.

When they arrived at the hospital, they were directed to the maternity waiting room where Jason and Martha were both pacing the floor from opposite directions. Jason stopped and walked into his mother's arms. "I'm so glad you're here. They haven't been out to talk to me for over an hour!"

Jason was small for a man, perhaps around 5-foot-10, and very slim. He had been scrawny as a child and hadn't filled out much as he matured. He had always been a good eater, but Sarah figured he burned up every calorie he ate. He was always on the go. At forty-one, despite a few gray hairs, he had the look of a much younger man.

"Why aren't you with her?" Sarah was surprised to find him in the waiting room. The two had been through all the classes in preparation for a natural delivery, and as the father and her coach, he was supposed to be with her.

"They took her into surgery," he responded frantically. "They had to do a cesarean at the last minute."

"Did they say why?" Sarah asked reaching out to him.

He pulled back, and running his fingers through his hair, responded, "They said something about fetal distress. If anything goes wrong ..." he began, but stopped and covered his face with both hands.

"Come sit down with me," Sarah said. "Charles, could you go down to the cafeteria and get us all a cup of coffee?"

"I'll go with you," Martha offered. She had remained in the background but ran her hand across her brother's shoulder as she passed behind him on her way to the door.

Once they were alone, Jason sat next to his mother and appeared to be holding back tears. Sarah took a tissue from her purse and laid it in his hand. His hair stood straight up on the top of his head, and Sarah smiled to herself remembering how he looked as a child struggling with his homework while running his fingers through his hair until it all stood straight up. "Tell me what the doctor said," she asked gently.

"It's the baby's heartbeat. The doctor said it was too slow."

"I don't think that's so unusual, Jason. And they took her right in for a C-section. They will both be fine, I'm sure." She wasn't as sure as she sounded, but Jason was clearly on the edge. He had lost his first son at the age of eleven and his first marriage ended as a result. Sarah knew Jason was reliving the loss of Arthur while worrying about Jennifer and their baby.

About that time, the doctor came into the room. "Mr. Miller?"

"Yes! Doctor, how is she?" Jason hurried across the room. "And the baby …?"

"They are both fine. You have a beautiful little girl, perfect in every way."

"Her heart?"

"Her heart is fine. She was distressed by the long labor, but she's recovered completely and is waiting to meet her new parents. Come on back."

"Mom?" Jason said looking back at this mother.

"I'll wait here. This is your time. Come get me when you're ready." Sarah had tears in her eyes, tears of relief and tears of joy. And tears for little Arthur who had been in the world for such a short time. Charles and Martha rushed to her side when they returned and saw her wiping her eyes.

"What happened?" Charles asked apprehensively.

"Nothing! They're both fine," she responded, laughing through her tears.

I'll never understand the emotional life of woman, Charles thought shaking his head as he took her in his arms.

He reached over and pulled Martha into their hug, and she laid her head on his shoulder. "I'm glad you're here," she said softly.

He patted the back of her head. "Me, too."

The group finally settled down and, drinking their coffee, speculated on what the couple might name their new little girl. Sarah and Martha ran through some of the family names, but they rejected most of them as being too old-fashioned. They didn't know any of Jennifer's family names. "If I'd had a girl, I would have named her Clementine," Charles said.

"She would never have forgiven you!" Martha responded with a snicker.

Sarah watched their playful exchange and was glad to see Martha warming up to her friends and the family. She wondered if anything would come of the budding friendship between Martha and Timothy. She liked Tim and could tell that Martha did too.

About that time, Jason stepped into the room and motioned for everyone to follow him. "Come meet my daughter," he said proudly. They followed him to the nursery where they spotted the little pink baby with her face scrunched up looking as if she couldn't decide whether or not to cry. Above her head was the hand printed sign, "Baby Girl Miller."

"I would like for you three to meet my daughter, Alaina Miller."

"Alaina?" Sarah said with pleased surprise. "What a pretty name!"

"It means *precious*, and that's just what she is, our precious little girl."

Later that night, they were able to see Jennifer for a short time. She was holding the baby in her arms, and Jason was standing close by in case she fell asleep again. She'd been having trouble shaking the effects of the anesthesia.

"I think we should go and let this new family spend some time alone," Sarah said. Martha and Charles immediately stood and began gathering their coats. Martha looked tired, Sarah noted.

Exhausted, the three headed for their cars. "Do you gals want to go somewhere for dinner?" Sarah and Martha agreed they were both too tired to eat. Martha got in her car and headed home while Sarah and Charles drove leisurely toward Cunningham Village. "It was a good day," Charles said reaching for Sarah's hand.

"You bet it was!" Sarah responded smiling. "A very good day." As they approached the house, a light snow began to fall.

Chapter 14

"Hi, Rhonda. I was surprised to see your name pop up on my caller ID. How are you?"

"I'm doing great, Martha. We miss you on the east coast, but it looks like you're doing a fantastic job with the Midwest office. We had a meeting last week with the Board, and they were duly impressed!" Martha smiled, knowing she had been very successful with her project.

"One little piece of *off-the-radar* news. I'm dating Malcolm," Rhonda announced.

"Malcolm Knight? I thought he was caught in Allison's web," Martha responded disdainfully.

"Well, that's another story. The reason I'm calling is to give you a message. You had a phone call from a lawyer out in Montana. He said it was personal."

"Hmm. That was probably Jackson Burns. Did he leave a message?"

"Just for you to call. He said it was urgent, though. That's why I'm calling. Do you have his number?" Martha and Rhonda continued to chat, but Martha was becoming tense wondering why Jackson was calling. "I'd better call

him now, Rhonda. Give my regards to the folks back there.
I miss them."

"Enough to come back?" Rhonda asked, already knowing
the answer.

"Absolutely not!" she responded confidently. "I'm where
I need to be."

Martha immediately dialed Jackson's number.

"Martha! Glad my message got to you so quickly. How
are you doing?"

"Fine. What's going on, Jackson?" she asked impatiently.

Speaking in a more serious vein, Jackson responded,
"I got word yesterday that Greyson was released last month."

"*What?* He was supposed to be in prison for another few
years, wasn't he?"

"It's been nearly twenty years, Martha. He was paroled
the first time he came up for a hearing. The guy that called
me said he's been a model prisoner."

"That's hard to believe. But what does this have to do
with me? We've been divorced for years."

"I just wanted you to know, that's all. He made threats
back then, and I thought you should know he's on the street."

"Thank you, Jackson. I appreciate the gesture, but he
won't be looking for me, not after all this time."

"Okay. Gotta run now, court in ten minutes. Good luck,"
and he hung up. Martha stood holding the receiver and
feeling contempt for the man who had caused her years of
unhappiness. *Surely he has moved on with his life*, she told
herself apprehensively. The black car crossed her mind, but
she immediately dismissed it. *He has no idea where I live*, she
reassured herself.

The phone rang again and she was hesitant to answer it. She decided to let it go to the machine but suddenly noticed the caller's name: Ward, Sophie. *Why would Sophie be calling me?* she wondered. Concerned that something might be wrong with her mother, she picked up.

"Well, hello there, lovely lady. I was beginning to think you weren't home."

"Hi, Tim!" She was relieved to hear his voice. They chatted for a while about the party and what he'd been doing since his arrival. He seemed to be dancing around something, and she decided to help him along. "So Tim. What's up?"

"I was wondering if you might like to go out to dinner Friday night?"

"I would enjoy that, Tim. Do you want me to meet you somewhere, or will you pick me up?" She was hoping he would be bringing her home since she was becoming wary of arriving home alone late at night.

"I'll pick you up if that's okay."

"That's perfect," she responded. She gave him her address and directions to her house, and they decided on an Italian restaurant on the outskirts of Middletown.

"Looking forward to it," he said as they hung up.

* * * * *

They were enjoying a leisurely meal and a bottle of wine. Martha was relaxed for the first time since the phone call with the attorney in Montana. "Tell me about Alaska. It sounds fascinating."

"Fascinating? Yes. And cold! And dark night and day for a few months up along the North Slope. But also it's lush and green in the summertime with pristine wilderness and free-roaming wildlife: bear, caribou, moose, mountain goats. You name it, we got it," he added with a chuckle as he refilled their wine glasses.

"How did you happen to go there?" Martha asked intrigued by what would motivate a young boy to make such an adventurous move.

"I guess it was mostly my science teacher. She was somewhat of a conservationist and she talked to us about the controversy over building the pipeline. Every day she read to us from the newspaper about the fights in congress and the environmental protestors who were trying to stop the pipeline. We were all intrigued by it. I had just graduated high school when the government gave their final approval in 1973. The oil companies were calling for workers and people were streaming to Alaska. My buddy Joe and I headed up there in his old jalopy. Once we got there, we found out they were only hiring locals and skilled workers, but we offered to work cheap and they agreed to give us a try."

"You were so young."

"Yeah? But I didn't feel young back then. We caught the train up to Fairbanks and from there they put us to work as laborers, building a gravel supply road the 360 miles on up to Prudhoe Bay where the pipeline started. Over the next few years, Joe and I worked in different camps along the line. I made friends with this one engineer, Randy. Randy Olson. Anyway, ol' Randy took me on and taught me the trade. He gave me my on-the-job engineering degree," he added with a chuckle. "By the time the pipeline was finished, I had worked at twenty-three of the twenty-nine pipeline camps at one time or another. Now I do maintenance, you know, looking for faults and directing the guys who do repairs. It was an exciting job in the 70s, but now it's pretty routine."

"I saw a picture of the pipeline the other day online. I was surprised to see it was built aboveground."

"Only about half of it. In some places, the earth is frozen and, if the pipe had been buried like they usually do, the hot oil would melt the ice and the line would be unstable." Tim started to tell her about the terrain but first asked, "Am I boring you?"

"Absolutely not! I'm fascinated by it."

"Well, I just wanted to add that the 800 miles of pipeline goes over rivers and streams and across three mountain ranges. It's a monumental achievement, and it was completed in just three years once it was finally approved. And the pay was great!" he added laughing. "Really great back in the 70s. Those oil guys were determined to get it done fast."

Timothy signaled for the waiter and turned to Martha. "Would you like dessert or coffee?"

"I'd love both, thank you."

"Okay, so that's all I'm going to say about me tonight and I really hope I haven't talked your ear off. Tell me about you."

Martha told him as much as she could about her job and then turned to her time in California. She didn't mention Montana or Greyson. She realized her story must sound very tame to this man who lived on what must feel like the edge of the world.

They finished their coffee and dessert and agreed it was time to head home. On the way, Timothy took a sudden turn off the main highway. "Why are you turning here?" Martha asked. "My turn is another mile up the road."

"I know. I'm being crazy, but that car has been on my tail since we left the restaurant. I just wanted to see what would happen if I turned off." As they made the turn, Martha saw the black car whiz past them.

"See?" he said. "I knew I was being crazy. They kept right on going, paying us no attention at all. I'm usually not this paranoid," he said apologetically as he reached over and patted her hand. "I had fun tonight," he added.

"So did I," she responded, trying to sound relaxed and unconcerned about the black car.

As they approached her house, she scoured the neighborhood, but there was no sign of the car. He walked her to her door and, again, gave her a quick kiss on the cheek as he turned to leave. She slipped into the house and locked the door. She heard him start his car and drive away. She heard another car pull up to the curb and stop. She heard the door open and slam closed. She heard footsteps.

Martha trembled as she leaned against the door waiting for the sound of the doorbell, but there was silence. She hadn't turned the lights on, so she crept through the darkness up the stairs and across her bedroom to the front window. She pulled the curtain aside only to see a car with a flashing neon sign on the roof that read *Pizza Guy*. A young boy was running toward the car from her neighbor's house carrying his empty pizza tote. Seconds later, he drove away.

"What's wrong with me?" she admonished herself aloud, knowing that the news about Greyson had her on edge.

Chapter 15

"Where's lover boy today?" Sophie asked trying to look innocent as she took her coat off and tossed it over Sarah's couch. "That was some pretty passionate kissing I saw on your front porch last night."

"Don't start," Sarah responded.

"But …"

"No. We aren't going to talk about it. Do you want coffee?"

"Sure, but …"

"Sophie!"

"Okay. I can mind my own business."

"That'll be the day," Sarah muttered as she turned the corner into the kitchen. Sophie followed her, and Barney opened his eyes suddenly when he realized that another member of his *pack* had arrived. They greeted each other, and Sophie headed for his treat container.

"Just one," Sarah announced in a gruff tone.

"Love doesn't become you," Sophie proclaimed. "It seems to be making you very grumpy!"

"Humph," Sarah responded with a slight smile.

"That's my line!" Sophie retorted.

Sarah didn't want to admit to herself that she and Charles had arrived at a new point in their relationship, so she sure didn't want to admit it to Sophie. She had lots of thinking to do. Charles wanted to get married. How could she possibly deal with this turn of events? She had no idea what to say to him, and she knew he was waiting for a response. With the excitement of the new baby, she had managed to avoid the topic, but she knew that wasn't fair to him. *It's cowardly*, she told herself. And yet, she didn't know what to say to him.

The two women sat down for coffee. Sophie honored Sarah's request that they not talk about Charles. Sophie asked about the baby and said she would like to go with Sarah to see her as soon as Jennifer felt like having company.

"We'll go next week." They talked about Jennifer and the baby and about the shop. They talked about Barney, the sale at Mulligan's Department store, and when Ruth would be back home. Then they sat silently.

"Okay, Sophie. I know what you want to know, so I'll tell you, but this isn't for *publication*. Charles asked me to marry him."

"*What?*" Sophie responded jumping up out of her chair with surprise.

"What did you say?"

"I didn't say anything."

"Nothing?"

"Well, I said something and I don't know just what. But I didn't say yes or no. I just said I would have to think about it."

"How romantic," Sophie said sarcastically as she flopped back into the chair.

"Look, Sophie. I don't expect you to understand this, but I'm not sure I'm ready for marriage."

"Oh, I can understand that. You've only been alone for twenty-some years … it takes time," again responding with her sarcastic tone.

"I don't see you getting married," Sarah retorted.

"I've only been alone for seven years. It takes time as I said. Besides that's different."

"How's that different?"

"I don't have a handsome man who adores me and is pleading for my hand in marriage."

They remained quiet for a while each buried in her own thoughts. A few minutes later, Sophie stood up and hobbled to the living room to get her coat. As she was leaving, she turned and looked at Sarah. "If you need to talk, come over. I care about you, kid."

"I know you do." Sarah walked closer to Sophie but held back, knowing that Sophie was not a hugger. She winked instead and said, "Thanks."

* * * * *

"Do you believe in long engagements?" Sarah asked.

Charles had just answered the phone excited to see that it was Sarah calling. Her greeting caught him off guard though.

"Do I believe in long engagements? Well, I guess I never thought about it," he responded. "Why do you ask?"

"Because if you do, I might say yes to your proposal. But only if we're talking about off in the future."

"How far off?" he asked, glad she couldn't see the smile on his face.

"Oh … say, maybe sometime next year?"

"Hmm. I guess I could go along with that if I had a definite *yes* to keep me going."

"Well, I don't want to accept your proposal on the telephone so please come over right away."

"You bet I'll be there right away before you have a chance to change your mind!"

"And then can we drive over and see the baby?" Sarah asked.

"Of course, we can. And then dinner at that Italian place out on Route 39 to celebrate?

"Perfect!" Sarah hung up the phone with a sigh. *What am I doing?* She realized she was shaking. She didn't know why she had been so reluctant to make a commitment to this dear man whom she loved and who loved her. She looked at herself in the mirror and saw that she was flushed. "I'm going to be engaged," she said aloud. "Seventy years old and engaged!" She laughed with joy but realized there were tears in her eyes.

I hope you understand, Jonathan.

Chapter 16

The phone was ringing when Martha returned home. It was Sunday, and she had made a special trip into the shop in order to transfer some data onto a thumb drive so she could do some troubleshooting at home. She hurried to answer the phone recognizing the number as one of the company lines.

"Hello, this is Martha."

"Martha. It's Davis. Sorry to bother you on the weekend but we have a problem here. We can't find the Donavan file. We need the results of the research they did down in Atlanta. Did you take the file home with you?"

"Of course not, Davis. I'm not involved in that project, at least not until you folks submit your department's report. Did it get misfiled?" She was immediately sorry she said that since, obviously, he wouldn't be calling her until all avenues had been pursued.

"We've looked everywhere, Martha. The entire file is missing, and this data hasn't been entered on the computer yet. We can always contact Donavan and get it re-transmitted, but I think we need to know what happened to it."

Martha knew that was true. This was critical data that could cost the company millions if it got out. "I'll give Alan a call. He might know something about it. I'll get back to you." She quickly dialed Alan's home number.

"Fitzgerald's residence." Martha was surprised by the formality and wondered if Alan had a housekeeper.

"May I speak with Alan please?"

"Who's calling?" the woman responded in a cool tone.

"This is Martha Miller from the office. Is Alan in?"

"This is his wife. May I ask why you want to speak with him?"

Taken aback, Martha responded, "We have a problem at work, and I need to ask him a question."

"You know, it's Sunday. You folks have him six days a week from early morning until late at night. My husband needs his rest. Is this really important?"

"Mrs. Fitzgerald. I'm truly sorry to bother you and Alan, but I only need to ask him one quick question." Without responding, Alan's wife laid the phone down.

Martha heard raised voices in the background but couldn't make out what was being said. After a long pause, Alan picked up the phone. "Martha. Sorry to keep you waiting. What's up?" He, too, sounded brisk.

Martha explained about the missing file. Alan expressed surprise and said he had no idea where it might be. "Donavan said they were transmitting it a few days ago. Are you sure we received it?" he asked.

"Yes. It was logged in on Thursday."

After reiterating that he had no information about the file, Alan said goodbye and hung up. Martha was surprised by his seeming lack of concern. Usually he was very cooperative and would have offered to go in and help the weekend staff locate the file. She wondered if he was having problems at home.

Putting the issue aside for the time being, Martha prepared an early dinner and spent the evening going over the figures from the shop. Her mother had said that Ruth might be coming home within the next few weeks, and Martha wanted the finances to be pristine for her. She went to bed early and read until midnight. Just as she turned her light off, she heard a car pull up outside. Most of her neighbors were elderly and were rarely out this late.

Leaving the light off, she slipped out of bed and went to the window. Carefully pulling the curtain aside, she looked out and spotted the car parked across the street. She saw the door slowly open, but the inside light had been deactivated. A figure quickly ducked out of the car and into the bushes directly across the street from Martha. She could barely make out the glow of a cigarette.

Shaking, she picked up the phone and called the police.

"Officer Muldoon. What's your emergency?"

"I want to report a prowler. There's a person outside my house in the bushes. Can you send someone over right away?" Martha's voice was trembling.

"He's on your property?" the officer asked.

"No. He's across the street," Martha replied. "But he's been here before." She was very nervous and didn't think she was being clear. "I think he's been following me."

The officer hesitated and then said, "I'll send someone out. Let me confirm your address." In about ten minutes, Martha heard a police car pull up in front of her house. She went to the window and saw that the black car was gone, and a female officer was getting out of the squad car followed by a young male officer. She met them at her front door and explained that the car was now gone. The officers checked the perimeter of her property and that of the neighboring houses. Someone opened their front door, but the officer told them to remain inside.

Once they confirmed that there was no one lingering around the house, they came in to talk with Martha. The young female officer's name was Officer Holmes, and she patiently listened as Martha told her and her partner about her misgivings regarding the black car.

"Do you know who it is?"

"No."

"Do you have any suspicions?"

Martha hesitated. "My ex-husband was recently released from prison in Montana. ..."

"Do you have reason to think it might be him?"

Again, she hesitated. "He threatened me during his trial, but that was nearly twenty years ago. I don't think it could be him." Office Holmes pulled out her notebook and asked a few questions about Greyson, most of which Martha couldn't answer.

"Is Greyson his first or last name?"

"As far as I know, it's his only name. He was born on a commune back in the early 70s. His mother was a hippie, and he never knew his father. He told me she named him Greyson. Just Greyson," she added with a shrug. "That's why I kept my maiden name."

"Some strange names came out of that decade." Moving on, Officer Holmes asked, "Do you have any other ideas about who it might be?"

"I fired a man a couple of months ago, and he was upset by it, but ..."

Officer Holmes turned to her notebook and asked for his name and the circumstances of the firing. She told the officer about the letter he sent her but didn't tell her about having dinner with him. She felt guilty about it, knowing she shouldn't have agreed to meet him. "Do you have the letter?"

"No. I threw it out. But I really don't think it's important. I'm sure it wasn't Derek."

"Stalking can be very serious, ma'am. You need to let us decide what's important."

Stalking? She hadn't thought of it as stalking. The idea was frightening, and she began to back away from the idea. "It's probably just my imagination," she said.

They continued to ask questions for the next half hour or so. The whole thing was beginning to feel out of control, and she was sorry she had involved the police. Finally, Office Holmes stood to leave. She handed Martha her card, and instructed her to call the direct number if she thought of anything else or if she saw the car again. Martha walked them to the door and promised to call.

Looking at the card after they drove off, Martha frowned slightly. *Amanda Holmes.* The name sounded familiar. Her mother, perhaps, had mentioned her. She would like to ask but didn't want to explain why the police were at her house.

Martha went to bed but had a restless night filled with troubling dreams she couldn't quite remember.

The next morning, she was exhausted but went into the office early. Alan was already there and greeted her in his usual friendly manner as if they hadn't had the uncomfortable conversation the night before.

In her office, she removed her boots and hung her coat up on the coat rack. She unlocked her desk and opened the drawer where she kept her current projects.

On the top of the pile lay the Donavan report.

Chapter 17

Over the next two weeks, staff from the New York office descended on the Middletown branch. Martha was questioned extensively as were all of her staff, but Martha seemed to bear the brunt of the allegations.

"I have no idea how that report got into my desk or where it was while it was missing," she responded angrily to the incessant questioning. "You know I'm a loyal employee and have been for years!" Martha was both hurt and angry that the blame for this was falling on her.

"If there's a corporate mole at work here," she snapped after an especially long interrogation toward the end of the first week, "you're missing the opportunity to catch him while you waste your time questioning me."

Before the investigator could respond, she added, "And why would you think this had anything to do with corporate espionage anyway? Maybe it was a simple mistake."

Nevertheless, the questioning continued, not just of Martha but of all her staff. "That was an especially grueling interview," Alan said as he joined Martha at Barney's, the local bar and grill where they had decided to meet to discuss what was going on. No work was getting done, and Martha was becoming worried about impending deadlines.

"Am I crazy to think this is a simple mistake? Do you think we have a mole?" she asked Alan.

"I have no idea. I've asked the corporate suits if there's been other evidence of a problem, but I don't get anywhere."

"I'm asking the questions here," Martha said, mimicking the corporate interviewers. "I'm sick of the whole thing. They are pulling personnel files now, and they have a subpoena to look at our staff's personal finances."

"Why in the world would they do that?" Alan responded indignantly.

"They're looking for people with outside income, people who seem to have two employers, us and someone hoping to ruin us."

Alan didn't respond but downed his whiskey in one gulp. "I heard they downloaded our hard drives to a special server so they could poke through our research and communications."

They decided to order sandwiches and return to the office to see if they could get some of the reports done for the upcoming meeting with their primary client. "We'll have to request a delay in the final report. There's no way we can complete the research with all the interruptions and the staff in a state of high anxiety."

They worked until nearly midnight and decided to call it a day. Alan walked her to her car and then slid into his Acura. He flashed his lights at her as he drove away.

Martha started her own car quickly, but as she was pulling out of her parking space, she spotted a car parked across the lot in the shadows. She turned and slowly drove in the direction of the car, but the car accelerated suddenly and its tires squealed as it sped toward the exit and out of sight. She couldn't see it clearly in the dark, but Martha knew it was the black car.

Martha didn't know who was stalking her, if it could even be called *stalking*. Sometimes she even thought it was just her imagination. *There are lots of black cars in this city*, she told herself. She also told herself she had no idea who it might be, but whenever she saw the car or received the calls, Derek's cold angry eyes crossed her mind.

On her way home, Martha toyed with a new idea. Both Derek and Greyson had crossed her mind as people who might want to make her uncomfortable or even fearful. But what if it had something to do with the company? She hadn't told anyone about the black car other than the skeptical police officers. *Maybe I should discuss it with Alan*, she thought tentatively.

Weeks earlier it had occurred to her that perhaps she should discuss it with Charles, but she immediately abandoned the idea, knowing that involving him would bring the family into it, and she was adamantly opposed to causing them any undue stress. *Yes, I think I should talk to Alan.*

* * * * *

"You look tired, Martha. Why don't you go on home. I can finish up here." Sarah had been helping Anna with a class while Martha handled the customers. Sarah had looked up to see Martha rubbing her temples with her eyes closed.

Quickly dropping her hands to her sides, Martha responded, "I'm okay, Mother. I can stay until closing time."

"Anna's here, Martha. Go on home. You need rest and tomorrow is Sunday. You can sleep in and …"

"Not tomorrow. We're working all day tomorrow. We have a big meeting this week with our primary client and we're far from ready."

"I'm sorry, Martha. You didn't have to be here today. I wish I had known, I would have insisted you take today off."

"I like being here," Martha responded in a soft tone.

"Are you really okay?" Sarah asked, moving closer to Martha and reaching out to touch her arm. Martha turned into her mother's arms, and tears ran down her face. "What is it, honey? Tell me."

"Just stress, Mama. Just stress. I'll be fine. You're right, I need rest. I guess I'll go on home if you're sure. …"

"I'm sure." Sarah helped her daughter gather up her coat and gloves and walked her to the door.

As Martha pulled away from the curb, Sarah noticed a car start up suddenly and swing in behind her daughter almost hitting her bumper. Sarah frowned and watched until the two cars were out of sight. She hurried to the phone and left Martha a message to call her as soon as she got home.

* * * * *

"I'm fine, Mother. I didn't even notice the car." Martha quickly changed the subject. "Are you about ready to go home?"

"Yes, but I was worried about you."

"Well, I'm home safe and sound and about to soak in a hot tub," Martha responded cheerfully.

"That's just what you need! I'll talk to you later in the week. I love you," and Sarah hung up, feeling relieved that it was nothing. *I hope I'm not starting to overreact like Charles does*, she told herself with a chuckle.

Martha hung up the phone and sighed. The car had followed her until she turned into her street, but didn't turn when she did. It was dusk and a thick fog had settled over the town making it impossible to determine who was driving the car. She drove slowly trying to get a look at the license plate. She could make out an *E* and what appeared to be a six. "E6," she said aloud, but the rest of the number seemed to be smudged, apparently with mud.

She drove around to the alley and entered her house from the back. Without turning the lights on, she went to the window. The car wasn't there. She was relieved but realized she was trembling anyway. She was tired of this constant feeling of foreboding.

"Those were the only two numbers I could make out," she explained to Officer Holmes when she called her later that night.

"I'll see what I can find out," the young officer said, but they both knew that was little to go on and, in fact, no crime had been committed. At least, not yet.

Chapter 18

It was Monday morning, and Ruth had just pulled into her familiar parking place in the alley next to Stitches. She had returned over the weekend and was eager to get back to the shop and resume her own very comfortable routine. Her mother had died the previous week, and Anna and her family had driven to Ohio for the funeral. Nathan, Ruth's husband, picked up Katie at school and the two drove straight to Ohio as well. It was the first time Katie had seen the house and the community where her mother grew up.

Ruth had been nervous about how the community would respond to their presence, but everyone was kind and comforting. It had been a very special experience to be able to be with her family and to care for her mother, but she was overjoyed to be home again.

As she unlocked the door, she smiled to see the shop just as she left it. Being in the shop brought back a feeling of being grounded for the first time since her mother died. She had felt somehow unattached or *free-floating*. It was as if an invisible umbilical cord connecting her to her mother had been cut.

Ruth had no sooner removed her boots and hung up her coat when she heard the jingle of the door being opened. She stuck her head out of the back room and was surprised to see all the members of the Friday night club crowding into the shop. Anna said good morning as she hurried past her sister carrying a large tray of sweet rolls.

Ruth rushed out to meet her friends, and was immediately inundated with hugs, questions, condolences, and a few tears. Ruth had missed her friends and they clearly had missed her as well. Sarah stood in the background, allowing Ruth to wallow in the lavish attention she was receiving.

"Sarah," Ruth called to her friend. "How can I ever thank you? The shop looks wonderful." She hurried over to Sarah, and they hugged and talked briefly about the shop.

"Let's set business aside for a few minutes," Anna interjected as she re-entered the room and the group became quiet. "Sarah, would you do the honors?"

"Me?"

"Yes, you," the group chimed in unison.

"What's this all about?" Ruth asked, looking around questioning.

"Okay," Sarah said. "Let's move into the classroom for coffee and refreshments, and while we're there, Ruth, we have a little surprise for you."

"Wait for me!" The voice came from the front of the shop, and the group turned to see Martha hurrying toward the classroom. "Am I in time?"

"Martha! You came!" Sarah introduced her daughter to the group, but most of the women had met her in the shop.

"So this is Martha," Ruth said hugging her and thanking her for all her work. "I haven't had a chance to see your reports, but your mother has been bragging about the work you've done."

"Maybe we'll have time to take a look at it before I leave. I don't need to be back to the office for a couple of hours. So," turning to her mother, "am I too late?"

"You got here just in time."

"What are you girls talking about?" Ruth asked impatiently.

"Anna," Sarah began, "helped us with a special project and," as she reached under the table and pulled out the bag, "we made this for you while you were away." She handed the bag to Ruth who took it gingerly with a look of confused anticipation.

"What did you gals do?" she asked rhetorically as she began opening the bag. Suddenly she gasped. "*Oh!* This is magnificent!" she squealed as she removed the quilt. She opened it out to its full size and spread it across the table, "Oh my! This is beautiful. And it reminds me of home!"

"That was our intention, Ruth. This is to remind you of your Amish home."

"… and it was our way of feeling close to you while you were away," Anna added.

Ruth gently ran her hands over the quilt with tears in her eyes. "This is so special. In fact, this reminds me of one of the first quilting bees I attended when I was young, maybe around nine or ten. My cousin was getting married soon, and we were helping her make the quilts she would take to her new home. One of the quilts looked very much like this one, and I was allowed to work on it. I remember my fingers were trembling, I was so afraid I was going to mess it up," she added laughing.

Looking at the simple nine-patch design, Anna realized that it was a very utilitarian quilt, and she wondered if they should have made something fancier, but knowing her sister, this was probably just right. The bright, cheerful colors reminded her of Ruth's shop and the black border spoke of her Amish background. *Yes, it's just right*, she reassured herself.

The group enjoyed the refreshments and talked excitedly about their next projects. Ruth and Martha slipped out to the back room and looked at the spreadsheets Martha had created. "I love this," Ruth said as she clicked around to see the various elements. "I can see other uses for this. Thank you, Martha. I want to pay you for all your time."

"Absolutely not!" Martha responded. "You did me a favor. It's been so good for mother and me to have this experience together. I've loved every minute of it, and you just might see me around here a lot more often. I think my mother is interested in teaching a beginning class, but she'll talk to you about that. If she does, I just might surprise her by signing up for the class."

"Oooh! That would be wonderful," Ruth responded, clapping her hands together. Ruth's words were cheerful and happy, but Martha detected a deep sadness in her eyes. She wondered what it must be like to watch one's mother die. She briefly thought about her own mother but immediately pushed the thought out of her mind. She knew the day would come, but she preferred to pretend it would never happen. Ruth saw the shadow cross Martha's face and laid her hand gently on her shoulder. The two women walked back into the shop having shared a meaningful but unspoken moment.

* * * * *

"Hi, Sheila. Where's Alan? And why's my door closed?" It was lunchtime and Martha had just returned to the office from Stitches. She was walking toward the door and was reaching for the doorknob when Sheila stopped her.

"Just a minute, Martha." Martha turned to her administrative aide questioningly. "Alan's wife is in there with Alan. I hope you don't mind. They needed a place to talk privately, and I didn't think you would be back until after lunch," Sheila explained apologetically.

"That's fine. I need to speak with Davis, so I'll head down to his department." As she turned to leave, she heard raised voices coming from her office and wondered what was going on. She hoped she would have a chance to meet the woman married to her handsome assistant.

When she returned sometime later, Alan had returned to his desk. He greeted her but without the usual enthusiasm. She stopped at his desk, and they spoke briefly, but he made no reference to his wife's visit. Later in the day, he stopped by her office to say he wouldn't be working late that night. Martha was surprised considering the impending deadline but knew there must be an important reason. He was always conscientious and willing to give his all to the job.

As Martha left the office late that night, the sky was overcast and there were no stars visible. She glanced around and was pleased to see her car was the only one in the lot. As she pulled away, however, she had the uncomfortable feeling she was being watched.

Chapter 19

"I don't feel like a new grandmother," Sarah complained to Sophie over coffee. "I've hardly seen little Alaina, and she's two months old already!"

"Oh my," Sophie responded, rolling her eyes. "She'll be going away to college soon."

"Oh, Sophie! I'm serious. While I was working at Stitches, I just didn't take the time to visit the baby. It's my fault, and I feel bad about it." She took a sip of her coffee but suddenly put the cup down and looked up resolutely. "I think I'll call Jenny and see if I can drop by this afternoon. Would you like to go with me?"

"Love to! Here's my cell phone. Give her a call." Sarah dialed and Jennifer answered sounding frazzled.

"Are you okay?" Sarah asked. "You sound out of breath. Did I call at a bad time?"

"No, Mother Miller. It's not that. I haven't had sleep for what feels like a year. This baby is adorable all day long, but she cries all night! I'm just beside myself. I need sleep!" Jennifer's voice was strained, and she sounded anxious.

"I was going to ask if I could come see you two this afternoon, but it doesn't sound like a good time for a visit." Sarah waited for a response, but the line was quiet. "Wait! I have an idea! Why don't Sophie and I come over and take care of her this afternoon, and you take a nice hot bubble bath followed by a long nap. How does that sound?"

"It sounds heavenly! Would you really do that?"

Sarah looked at Sophie and raised her eyebrows questioningly. Sophie shrugged and said "Why not."

When they arrived, Jennifer met them at the door with her coat in her hand. "Are you going out?" Sarah asked, looking surprised.

"I'm going to do just what you suggested, a bubble bath and a nap, but I'm going to do it at my mother's house! If I stay here, I'll be constantly listening for Alaina and getting up to see if she needs me. Do you two think you can handle this?"

Sarah assured Jenny they would be fine but asked her to show them where everything was before she left. Jenny had written everything down for them including her phone numbers and Jason's just in case. Despite being eager to get time for herself, when it came to actually walking out the door, Jennifer had trouble. "Are you sure you'll be okay?" she asked again as she came back and kissed Alaina's cheek for the third time.

"Go!" Sophie ordered. Once Jennifer's car pulled out of the driveway, Sophie turned to Sarah and asked, "What does a baby this age do?"

"Not much I don't think. Let's just sit down with her on my lap for now and see how it goes." Within minutes, Alaina began to get fussy. The two women looked at each other, and Sarah said, "Let's check her diaper." Sure enough, the diaper needed changing, and the three headed for the baby's room upstairs.

While Alaina was lying on the change table, she seemed to be focusing on a colorful mobile that was hanging above her. Sarah reached up and pushed the switch, which caused it to rotate and play a tune. Alaina flailed her arms and kicked her legs with excitement while watching the movement.

There was a portable carrier in the corner of the room and Sarah decided to put her in it and take her back downstairs. They went into the kitchen to make a pot of coffee only to discover the sink was full of dirty dishes. "Let's take care of these," Sophie said rolling up her sleeves and attacking the mess.

"I'll make coffee," Sarah said setting the carrier on the counter so Alaina could watch her. "Do you think she can see me?" she asked Sophie.

"I don't know, but people are always getting really close to a baby's face. Maybe they can only see up close." Sarah moved the carrier closer. "I think she just smiled at me."

"Have you totally forgotten about babies? You raised two of them. That's no smile, friend." Moments later, Sarah was carrying the baby upstairs for yet another diaper change.

When she returned to the kitchen, she didn't have Alaina. "Where's the baby?"

"She was yawning, so I put her in her crib, and she went right to sleep." Sarah found cleaning supplies and did a thorough cleaning of the kitchen and the downstairs bathroom while Sophie did the dishes. By the time the baby woke up, the living room had been vacuumed and dusted. "I hope Jenny doesn't mind that we did this."

"How can she mind? You go get the baby, and I'll warm up a bottle," Sophie said.

Alaina spent the next hour downstairs with Sophie and Sarah taking turns holding her. Sarah especially enjoyed walking around the house carrying her and softly singing. Alaina lay quietly in her arms and stared at her, appearing to be memorizing the face of her grandmother. Sarah noticed she was always quiet while she was singing and kicked noticeably when she stopped as if she were asking for more.

"I wish we could take her for a walk," Sarah said at one point.

"It's too cold out there for a baby," Sophie responded. "And it's too cold for me, too," she added. "My bones have ached all winter." Sophie's arthritis had been bothering her more than usual, especially her right knee. She was using her cane now all the time.

"What does the doctor say about your knee?" Sarah asked.

"Oh, he's just talking silly stuff."

"What do you mean?"

"You know. He talks about turning me into a robot with bionic parts."

"Are you talking about a knee replacement, Sophie?" Sarah asked, trying to get Sophie to be serious.

"I guess."

"And …?"

"And what? Am I going to do it? What do you think?"

"I think …" Sarah began.

"Stop! I decided I don't want to hear what you think. It will be the same as what the doctor thinks and what Timothy thinks. I'm going out of this world with all my body parts intact."

Alaina was becoming restless and had her face scrunched up on the verge of crying. "I think we may need another diaper change," Sarah said. "You stay down here. No reason you should climb those stairs in your condition."

"In my condition? Excuse me, friend, but I was the first one up those steps this morning." She grabbed her cane and hobbled to the stairway.

"Sophie, you are climbing the stairs too fast. Slow down." Sarah held her breath fearing that Sophie was going to tumble back down the stairs, but she made it to the top.

"Let's give her a bath," Sophie suggested when Sarah and the baby came into the room. "See? There's a little bathtub over there and a pot for carrying water. I'll sit down in the rocking chair and hold Alaina while you fill the tub." Sarah thought this was somewhat overstepping their role but agreed to do it.

As it turned out, they all three had a great time. Alaina kicked and splashed the water and even squealed once or twice. Once she was dried and powdered, they dressed her in a soft flannel nightgown. Sophie again held her in the rocker while Sarah cleaned up the splashed water and put the wet towels over the shower rod in the bathroom. Then she took the baby and walked her until she fell asleep in her arms.

"Now I feel like a grandmother again," Sarah said with a relaxed smile as they were driving home.

Chapter 20

"What do you think you're doing?"

Martha had picked up the phone without looking at the caller ID, something she rarely did. "Who is this?" she demanded.

"You know perfectly well who this is! The police were here yesterday questioning me about 'lurking around your house' as they put it. What's the meaning of this?" She realized it was Derek. His voice intensified until he was practically screaming into the phone. "You flirt with me shamelessly, you humiliate me in public, you ignore my letter, and now you lie about me to the police. What are you trying to do to me?"

Martha struggled for the right response. If Derek wasn't the stalker, she owed him some sort of explanation. If he were the stalker, she would be playing right into his hands by becoming defensive. She didn't speak.

"Martha!" he snarled angrily.

"Derek, if you want to discuss this with me, call Officer Holmes at the police station and arrange a time for the three of us to sit down and talk."

Derek slammed the phone down. Martha picked up Officer Holmes' card and dialed her number.

"Holmes," the officer answered.

"Officer Holmes, this is Martha Miller. You were at my house last week. ..."

"Yes, I remember. How can I help you?"

Martha told the police officer about her call from Derek Kettler and her suggestion about meeting at the police station. "Well," Officer Holmes responded, "that would be unusual, but I'm willing to do it. Generally, these kinds of meetings would be with your lawyer rather than the police department."

"I don't have a lawyer and don't think I need one. I just thought ..."

"It's fine, Ms. Miller. I'm willing to meet with him, but I doubt that he'll ever call. If he's your stalker, it's unlikely that he would walk into the police station."

Martha had no sooner hung up the phone that it rang again. This time she checked the caller ID and was pleased to see Sophie Ward's number displayed. She and Tim had been out to dinner several times since his arrival and were planning to go to the movie and dinner on Friday. "Hello," she answered cheerfully, setting her concerns about Derek aside.

"Hi, Martha. This is Tim Ward."

"It's good to hear from you, Tim." They chatted for a few minutes before he got to the point of his call.

"So," Tim said, "I was wondering if we could skip the movie next Friday and drive up to Hamilton instead? There's a new club up there with dinner and dancing and ..."

"That sounds wonderful," she responded enthusiastically. "I haven't been dancing since …" She couldn't finish the sentence because she realized she had never been dancing!

"I'll have to warn you," Tim confessed, "there's not much dancing going on along the Alaska pipeline. Wear shoes with protective armor!" They laughed and agreed they would both have challenges to overcome on the dance floor.

They chatted for a few minutes about what they had been doing when Tim said, "By the way, I just got off the phone with my boss up in Valdez. I talked to him about the possibility of retiring in the next year are so. I just might do it."

"I'm surprised," Martha responded. "You seem to love your work."

"I do, but I've been at it for over thirty years and my aging joints are beginning to show the wear," he responded with a chuckle. Then in a more serious tone, he added, "After spending some time down here with Mom, I'm beginning to see there's life outside of Alaska." Lowering his voice, he added, "Besides, I'm concerned about Mom. She's alone here and not in the best of health although she'd never admit that. I'd like to be closer to her."

"I understand what you're saying. The mother of one of Mom's friends just died, and it's making me appreciate the time I spend with my mother."

After they hung up, Martha caught herself smiling. She liked the idea of having Tim around. He was interesting and fun. Also, she liked that he was concerned enough about his mother that he would consider taking such a big step. As she put her dinner on the table, she caught herself hoping he would decide to retire. Much to her surprise, she was actually enjoying his company.

* * * * *

"Hi, Sarah. What are you up to today?" Ruth asked as Sarah entered the shop. "Are you starting another quilt?"

"No, but I wanted to talk with you about that beginning class we discussed. I was working up a potential curriculum and wanted to get your input."

Ruth read down the list of subjects Sarah was proposing: the parts of a quilt, choosing a pattern, choosing fabric, accurate cutting, and the perfect seam. "I thought we would do each of these steps while making a simple four-patch quilt, perhaps with sashing and one border," Sarah interjected when Ruth finished reading the list.

"A bed quilt?" Ruth asked tentatively.

"No. I thought a throw would be easier for new quilters to handle."

"I think starting with a throw is a good idea. Something around 50″ by 70″ is an easy size to work with while you're learning. There aren't too many blocks to deal with, and it doesn't get heavy and unmanageable."

"So what do you think of my outline?" Sarah asked somewhat reticently, still reluctant to acknowledge she knew enough to teach a class.

"I think it's an excellent plan, and you'll be my most popular teacher in no time! How about early spring? Maybe we could advertise that the classes will meet weekly beginning in March?"

Sarah left the shop smiling. *Another new adventure!*

Chapter 21

"Absolutely!" Sarah responded to her daughter who had called early Saturday morning. "I'm sure Charles would be happy to give you a brush-up dancing lesson. He's a very good dancer, too."

Sarah was surprised by the request and tickled to think Martha would ask for Charles' help. She was also pleased that her daughter was showing some interest in social activities. Martha had told her that she wasn't romantically interested in Timothy Ward, but she was enjoying going out with him. She was especially intrigued by his stories of Alaska, and she was beginning to consider visiting there one day. "Maybe we could take an Alaskan cruise?" she had suggested to her mother one day.

"When do you think Charles would be able to do it? Tim has invited me to a club on Friday."

"He's coming for lunch today. How about you come too, and you and Charles would have the afternoon to work on it?"

"Perfect! But call Charles and make sure this is okay with him." Martha was concerned that her mother had referred to it as a brush-up lesson, considering she had never actually learned to dance at all. She had watched her mother and Charles dancing at Sophie's party, and he certainly knew what he was doing. She hoped she wouldn't make a fool of herself Friday night, *or this afternoon for that matter*!

Sarah had made minestrone and served it with sour dough rolls and a side salad. Halfway through lunch, Charles stood and said, "I think we need to make our afternoon just a little more festive. Let's open a bottle of wine." He headed for the refrigerator and removed a bottle of zinfandel. Martha noticed how comfortable he seemed in Sarah's kitchen and wondered how much time he spent there.

After lunch, they moved into the living room and Charles put a disk in the player. Instead of dancing, however, he sat down and asked Martha to tap her finger to the beat. He skipped to another melody and repeated the exercise, helping Martha listen to the music in a slightly different way. "You need to get beyond the melody and the words and listen to the beat." He then held out his hand and led her through a simple fox-trot as they repeated, "slow-slow-quick-quick, slow-slow-quick-quick." Martha felt stiff and anxious at first, but as Charles demonstrated the steps and expertly led her across the floor, she began to relax. She could feel his hand firmly guiding her, and she realized she was dancing with someone who knew what he was doing. She wondered whether Tim would be as skilled at leading, obviously an important component in dancing.

Once she was comfortable with the fox-trot, they spent some time on the waltz, and he even included a slow underarm turn. Martha was surprised at how she was able to flow with the music once she relaxed. "I like this!" she exclaimed after the initial awkward period. The hardest part for her was to allow Charles to lead. She was accustomed to being in charge, and once she learned the steps, she automatically moved into her take-charge mode.

"Relax and just let me lead," he repeated gently.

Charles was a patient teacher. Sarah watched from the sideline, feeling love for both of them and enjoying their interactions. *How could I have been reluctant to accept this man's proposal*, she wondered as she watched him guide her daughter around the makeshift dance floor.

They took several breaks and once Martha seemed comfortable with the steps, he demonstrated the cha-cha with Sarah, but it clearly frightened Martha to think Tim might expect her to be that skilled. "I don't think you'll have to worry about that," Charles assured her. "Tim doesn't strike me as a *cha-cha kind of guy.*" They all laughed as they pictured this hefty, bearded man lumbering around the dance floor in cha-cha mode!

On her way home, Martha turned the car radio on, something she rarely did. She dialed away from the all-talk news station, which was the only button she had set, and stopped on a soft music station. She found herself smiling as she thought about the afternoon. *I've missed so much*, she admitted to herself reluctantly.

She boldly parked in front of her house giving no thought to the black car. She pulled her mail from the box and went into the house but was surprised to feel a cold draft. Walking through the house toward the kitchen, she realized the back door was standing open. "How could that be?" she asked aloud. She closed and locked the door and tried to remember when she might have left it ajar, thinking that perhaps the wind had blown it open. Still troubled by it, she hung up her coat and checked around the first floor. Nothing was out of place. She went upstairs and gasped. Her dresser drawers were standing open and their contents strewn about.

She immediately called Officer Holmes but was told it was her day off. Two officers were sent to her house, but they found no evidence of a break-in. "The door was left open or opened with a key," one of the officers announced authoritatively. She assured him the door was *not* left open, and no one, to her knowledge, had a key. They dusted for fingerprints, but none was found. Nothing appeared to be missing. They questioned her about who might have been in her house, but it felt more like an interrogation, and she ultimately referred them to Officer Holmes. They seemed a bit disgruntled when they left, and she had the feeling they were suspicious of her for some reason.

Once alone, Martha sat down on her bed and looked at her intimate apparel scattered around the room. *Had someone been looking for something? Or just trying to frighten me?* She felt alone. She knew she needed to talk with someone about the break-in and about the black car. *But who?* She had thought about talking with Alan about it, but something held her back. Then she thought about Tim, but he was leaving soon.

She wondered if Officer Holmes would be willing to sit down with her over coffee and talk about it, but she doubted that the young woman would have the time. She thought about Charles' and realized he was the perfect person to talk to, but she had been trying to keep her mother out of it. *But perhaps that isn't necessary. She's a strong woman. Maybe I don't need to protect her.*

She thought again about the break-in and the black car. *Were they related?* She didn't know, but she suspected they were. *Who is doing this?* She realized her hands were trembling.

Without giving it any more thought, she picked up the phone and dialed her mother quickly before she could change her mind. "Is Charles still there?" she asked.

"Yes, honey. He's here. Did you want to speak with him?"

"No. I was wondering if the two of you could come right over. I need you both." Her voice cracked on the word *need*, and her mother spotted it immediately.

"Are you okay?" her mother asked apprehensively.

"No, Mama, I'm not okay. I need you and Charles. Please come."

"Of course, we'll come! We'll be right there."

Chapter 22

"Why didn't you come to us sooner?" Sarah asked, distressed that Martha had kept this to herself. The three sat in Martha's living room while she told them about the black car and the police's theory that she was being stalked. Sarah added, "You could have been in danger...."

"She called us now, Sarah. Let's go over all the details, and we'll figure out a way to put an end to this," Charles said reassuringly. "Now start from the beginning."

"I'm not sure where it began. I'd been feeling like someone was watching me ... you know, that feeling that makes you look around, but then no one is there?" They both nodded but were eager for more of the story.

"The first time I noticed the black car," Martha continued, "was the night of Sophie's party."

"We picked you up that night. You didn't say a word...." Sarah began, but Charles gave her a look that clearly suggested she stop talking.

"I know. I'm sorry, but I really didn't suspect anything until the next week when Tim and I went out to dinner. A black car seemed to be following us when we left the restaurant."

"Tim saw it?" Charles asked.

"He saw it first, but he dismissed it when it didn't follow us once he turned off the main road. I was pretty sure it was the same car, but I didn't say anything to Tim."

After a short pause, Martha continued. "Then, let me see …" Martha hesitated, trying to reconstruct the order. "Yes! It was the next week that I saw the car pull up and stop a few doors up. Someone got out and stood behind the trees directly across the street."

"And you report …"

"Mom, I did! I called the police. They came out and looked around, but he was already gone."

"I know some of the older guys at the precinct. Do you remember who came out?" Charles asked.

"Two officers. One was a young woman, Officer Holmes."

"Amanda Holmes?" Sarah asked with surprise. "Amanda?"

"Yes! I thought I recognized her name. You know her, don't you?" Martha said, becoming animated for the first time that evening.

"We both know her," Sarah responded looking at Charles then back at Martha. "She's the one that helped us find Caitlyn last year. What did she say?" Sarah was clearly relieved now that she knew Amanda was involved.

"Well, the gist of it all is simply that no crime has been committed."

"This person can terrify you …?" Sarah began.

Charles spoke up. "The car is on a public street. The police didn't see him lurking around the house. He hasn't approached her. …" Turning to Martha he added, "He hasn't, has he?"

"We don't even know this is a *he*," she responded, "but no, he hasn't approached me."

"Okay, go on."

"Well, then the car followed me home from Stitches one day. ..."

"Wait! I saw that car! I called you and you said ..."

"Mother, I know what I said. I lied and I'm sorry. I wasn't ready to talk about it. I still wasn't sure whether I was imagining it, and I sure didn't want to worry you. Besides, he didn't follow me all the way home."

"But Wait!" Sarah said abruptly, looking excited. "I saw the license plate when he pulled up behind you!"

Martha and Charles both turned to Sarah astounded. "You saw the license?" Sarah reached for her purse and searched around until she located a scrap of paper. "Here it is, E6. ..."

"Is that all you saw?"

"Yes, but it's a beginning, right?"

Martha looked deflated as she sat back down. "I saw that much myself. I called Officer Holmes and told her, but it wasn't enough to go on. She said she would check it out, but she wasn't encouraging."

The three sat quietly for a few minutes.

"Anything else?" Charles asked.

"Yes. I haven't told you the worst part yet." Martha led her mother and Charles up the stairs to her bedroom and let them go in first. She saw her mother put her hand to her heart as she looked at the disheveled room.

"Oooh," Sarah muttered as tears sprung to her eyes. "I'm so sorry," she said, pulling her daughter into her arms.

"Okay. Now a crime has been committed!" Charles announced authoritatively. "We need to call the police...."

"I have. Amanda wasn't there, but they sent out two other officers." She handed their cards to Charles. "They weren't helpful. In fact, I'm not sure they even believed me. They couldn't find evidence of a break-in."

"I don't know these guys, but I'll check it out." Charles had been retired for six or seven years but still had friends on the force. In fact, he occasionally did work for his old lieutenant, Matthew Stokely. "I'll call Matt tomorrow and see what I can find out."

Sarah started to pick up some of Martha's clothing from the floor, but looked inquiringly at Charles. "Is it okay to move these?"

"Yes, the police have already investigated as much as they're going to. Go ahead. She needs her room." Together the three got things back in order, Martha and Sarah folding clothes and Charles putting the drawers back in the dresser. "Is anything missing?" he asked Martha.

"Not that I know of," she said distractedly. Her mind had returned to wondering who might be doing this.

An hour later, the three moved downstairs to the kitchen. Martha brewed tea while Sarah removed a package of cookies from the cupboard.

"Those might be stale," Martha said offhandedly.

"We'll dunk them if we need to," Sarah responded. Looking directly into her daughter's eyes, she added reassuringly, "We'll do whatever we need to do." This time Martha initiated the hug knowing her mother was no longer talking about the cookies.

"Thank you," she said gently.

The three sat for over an hour while Martha caught them up on her suspicions about Derek Kettler and possibly Greyson.

"I can check out this Greyson character. I'll call Probation and Parole in Montana and see what I can find out about this guy. What's the rest of this Greyson guy's name?" Martha again explained about his hippie mother and "Greyson" being his only name while Charles stared at her incredulously.

"Amazing," he responded, shaking his head. Getting back to the issue, he added, "Also I'll see if this Derek Kettler has a record."

"And I can talk to Amanda," Sarah interjected. "She comes to our Friday night quilt sessions occasionally, and we've become good friends. She'll be a good person to have on our team," Sarah added clearly getting excited about having another mystery to solve.

"Slow down," Charles said, looking at her with that look she so resented.

"Charles …?" she said with her eyebrows drawn high on her forehead.

"We'll talk later," he said somewhat dismissively. Sarah frowned. Martha hoped she wasn't responsible for stirring up problems between these two. Charles was very protective of her mother and her mother was very independent and resented his interference. She had told Martha she often felt smothered by him. *I hope I haven't caused trouble.*

"So," Charles said changing the subject and looking at Martha. "Did you see the car any other time?"

"Hmm. Well, I can't be sure, but I think it's been in the parking lot at work. A couple of times when I was leaving late, I thought I saw it, but it immediately took off. I couldn't really see the car all that well."

"Anything else?"

Martha hesitated. "Sometimes I feel like I'm being watched, but I can't swear to it. It's probably my imagination. I've been really tense about this and stuff that's going on at the office. ..."

"What stuff?" Sarah asked abruptly turning her attention to the conversation between Martha and Charles. "What stuff?" she repeated.

Martha signed deeply. "Okay. I guess I can tell you." She told them the situation with the missing report that turned up in her desk and about the investigation that was going on. "They seem to think I have something to do with it."

"Are you being set up?" Charles asked pointedly. Martha looked surprised and didn't answer right away.

"I don't know," she finally said tentatively. "I don't know."

Chapter 23

"Good Morning, Sheila." Martha was rarely late for work and felt compelled to offer an explanation to her administrative aide. "My car wouldn't start in the cold; it's probably the battery." She handed Sheila the business card from her mechanic and asked that she arrange for them to meet her there at noon.

"No problem. I'll call right away. Will you need a ride? I'd be happy to take you."

"Thanks, Sheila, but I already spoke with Alan. We have some reports to go over, and we can do that on the way." Martha went into her office and started to close the door but turned and asked Sheila if there had been any messages.

"Yes. You had a call from an Officer Holmes. I put the number on your desk. Is everything all right?" Sheila looked intrigued and was clearly eager to hear why Martha was being called by a police officer.

"Oh, that's Amanda. She's a friend." Martha paused and then added, hoping to downplay the importance of the call, "If she calls again, tell her I'll call her later." She didn't want to become any more of an item on the rumor mill than she already was. She knew people were talking about the number of times she'd been interrogated.

Once she got settled in her office, Martha picked up the phone, but instead of calling Amanda right away, she dialed Sheila's desk. "Sheila, would you get Rhonda Phillips for me." Rhonda had been a good friend and a tremendous support to her during her years in the east coast office. But, with the exception of the time Rhonda called her about the message from the attorney in Montana, the two friends had been out of touch for the last few years. Martha wasn't sure it was appropriate to call on her at this point, but she had to know what the scuttlebutt was back east.

"Martha, hi! I've been meaning to call you. What's going on out there anyway?"

"What do you mean?" Martha asked, hoping Rhonda would fill her in without her having to ask.

"All of us underlings out here can only speculate. No one's telling us a thing. We only know that corporate has sent out several investigators and our legal staff is going crazy. It looks like they are sealing up all the holes."

"What do you mean?"

"Well, what I heard was that Cordidyne's major competitor just leaked Middletown's negative test results to the press."

"What results? We're still in the preliminary phase. We don't have final results."

"Well, they made it sound final. They listed all the dangerous side effects. No one is ever going to buy this product if it even gets to the marketplace."

"Do they say where they are getting their information?"

"They're quoting your research word for word. I compared it with your last internal report. You have someone out there you can't trust."

Martha sat back in her chair and pushed her hair out of her eyes. She was baffled by what Rhonda was saying. *Who released this information?*

"What I heard," Rhonda continued, "is that they're tightening up security out there and continuing to investigate. They're determined to find the leak. Is that your unit, Martha? Your name keeps coming up. I've been worried. ..." she added as her voice trailed off.

"I have final sign-off on it, but the work is being done in Davis' lab. I'm following it, of course." *Alan and I are following it*, she thought but didn't say.

After she hung up, she realized the back of her blouse was damp from a nervous sweat that had washed over her during the call. *Alan?* Alan was new to the corporation and where had he come from? He'd been hired by corporate, so she didn't have his original paperwork. *But, they are looking at me, not Alan.*

The trip back to her house at noon was tense and awkward. "Are you okay?" Alan asked.

"I'm just worried about the car," she responded. She had planned to tell Alan about the stalker and ask if he thought it could be related to the work they were doing, but now? Could she trust him? She had no idea. Did he know about the news release? Should she ask him? Her thoughts were muddled and confused. She remained quiet.

Alan looked at her with what appeared to be honest concern. "Martha, relax. It's probably just your battery. It's been really cold and your car sits out."

How does he know my car sits out? When has he ever ... but then she realized this isn't the first time he has driven her home. During the first weeks he was with the company, he had offered to help on several occasions during the period she was trading in her old Chevy. "You're probably right. It's probably the battery. I should stop buying used cars."

The tow truck was just pulling into her street when they arrived. Martha got out and waved to the driver; she then turned to Alan, thanking him for the ride and assuring him she would be fine. She wasn't sure how she'd get back to work if the car didn't start, but she didn't want to keep up the facade with Alan. He shrugged and reluctantly drove off.

As suspected, it was the battery, and within a couple of hours Martha was back in the office. She immediately closed her door and pulled out her schedule. She had missed a meeting with her own staff which Sheila had taken the initiative to cancel, knowing Martha would be out. She decided to take the time to call Officer Holmes.

"Holmes," the officer answered.

"Officer Holmes, this is Martha Miller returning your call."

"I'm glad you called," she responded enthusiastically. First of all, when I met with you a few weeks ago, I had no idea you were Sarah's daughter. Sarah and I've become great quilting friends. She didn't tell me a thing about your situation until today!"

"That's because she didn't know. I just told her about it. Did she call you?"

"Yes, and I'm glad she did. She filled me in on what happened recently. I pulled the reports and would like to come over and talk with you. When would be a good time for you?"

Martha said she could be free whenever the officer wanted to come, and they decided on that evening after work. "Would it be okay to have mother and Charles there too?" Martha asked.

"It's fine with me as long as you can speak freely in front of them. I really need to know the entire story."

"That's not a problem anymore, and I'm sorry now that I kept it from them for so long. They are being very supportive. ..."

"You can't go wrong with those two on your side!" Amanda said laughing. "I'll see you tonight."

Chapter 24

"So our children are dating, my Timmy and your Martha. What will that make us if they get married?" Sophie was sitting with Sarah in the café and biting into a cream-filled cherry Danish as she asked the question.

"I guess we'd be in-laws of some sort, but that scenario is very unlikely. My Martha is quite down on men right now."

"Including my Timmy?" Sophie asked indignantly as she wiped the cream off her chin.

"Well, maybe not *your* Timmy specifically, but the male species in general."

"How did the meeting with Amanda go?"

"Charles and I mostly listened while Martha caught Amanda up on all the details about Greyson and Derek. Then she told her about this mess at her work, most of which I was unaware of."

"What's going on?"

"It's not clear. Someone has leaked critical information to the press and they have been looking closely at Martha."

"Martha! Why Martha?"

"There was something about a missing file, and last week they got in a tailspin when they discovered the $25,000 I had given her from my inheritance."

"What do they care?"

"They didn't believe her story about where it came from. Martha told me they're looking for evidence that someone is being paid by a competitor. I had to go into a lawyer's office and show proof of the transfer. They even wanted *me* to verify where *I* got the money!"

"The nerve!" Sophie huffed as she broke off a piece of Sarah's untouched Danish. "But what does all this have to do with the stalker?"

"Amanda is just trying to identify anyone who might have a reason to be following Martha. She seems to think it might all be related."

"So, what are we going to do to get to the bottom of this mess?" Sophie asked, pushing her plate away and looking eager to get started playing detective.

"Charles said that we are absolutely not to get involved in the investigation. He even got Amanda to side with him. They both said 'leave this to the professionals!'"

"Humph! So where do we start?" Sophie responded, totally ignoring Charles' and Amanda's restrictions.

"I was thinking we could follow Derek. That way we can determine ..."

"You can determine *what?*" the deep voice approaching the table bellowed.

"Oh! Hi, Charles. We weren't expecting you."

"Obviously! So, what is it you plan to determine by following Derek?" Charles was frowning and clearly displeased. Not giving them a chance to explain, he continued, "Didn't you listen to a word of what Amanda said? You two are to stay totally out of the investigation. Do you understand?"

Charles immediately knew he had gone too far. Sarah was glaring at him, and Sophie's feathers were clearly ruffled. "Now just a minute ..." Sophie started to speak, but Sarah interrupted.

"I will not be spoken to in that tone!" She stood and turned to Sophie, "Come on. We're leaving." With that, she headed straight to the door while Sophie flounced behind.

"Did you pay the bill?" Sophie asked.

"He wants to be the big man *in charge*? Well, he can pay the bill! Let's go to your house and plan our strategy. Do you think Tim will help?"

* * * * *

"So, Tim, how is it that you never got married?" Tim and Martha had returned to Larochelle's, the Italian restaurant that was quickly becoming their favorite dinner spot. It was a relief for Martha to get away from the company inter-rogators, Amanda's questions, her family's concerns, and especially the black car. She took a big sip of her wine and gazed at Tim, waiting for his response.

"Just never got the chance, I guess. Woman are scarce along the pipeline," then he added looking a little embar-rassed, "at least the marrying kind if you know what I mean."

"No girlfriends even?" Martha asked, continuing to press the issue.

Tim remained quiet at first but then sighed deeply. "Yes, there was this one girl. It was a long time ago, back when I was young. I was working the pipeline out of Fairbanks at the time, and Betsy did office work for the big shots."

"Tell me about her," Martha said, eager to know more about his life.

"She was born in Alaska. Her folks lived off the grid an hour or so south of Fairbanks by train. She and I hung out together for a couple of years enjoying the Fairbanks city life. I'd been pretty isolated up north in the construction camps before that." He hesitated and took a sip of his wine.

"What do you mean by 'off the grid'?"

"Off-gridders are those self-sufficient folks who decide to do it on their own. They move away from modern conveniences and live an isolated life off the land. Up in Alaska, some of the off-gridders build their cabins a mile or two from the train tracks."

"Why along the tracks?" Martha asked trying to picture life in such a remote place.

"That's so they can get around. There aren't that many roads, and they're often impassable in the winter. Off-gridders will walk or take snow machines out to the tracks. The Alaska Railroad passenger train will stop for them just like a bus would in the city. They ride up the tracks to the next town and get provisions or whatever and then catch the train back later that day."

"Anyway, we were together for a couple of years. A couple of times, I went with her to visit her folks. Once we stayed two weeks when her dad was sick. It's a hard life for sure."

"That's fascinating! Tell me what it was like out there."

"Well, they had a small cabin, just a couple of rooms. Solar panels and a wood stove. No electricity, of course. No plumbing. You're really roughing it to live like that.

Betsy seemed perfectly comfortable while we were there. I guess she grew up that way, but this ol' city boy had some problems with it." Martha liked the way he smiled from one side of his mouth when he talked.

"How did her folks manage out there all those years? Did her dad work?"

"He fished and hunted. They farmed in the summer and her mom canned food for the winter. We were there in the early fall, and they had the cold cellar full of canned food and the smoke house was packed with meat."

The waiter stopped at their table and they ordered coffee and dessert. Martha would have been happy to split something, but Tim was a voracious eater, so she ordered her own dessert, knowing he could eat his and part of hers, as well.

"I'm having trouble picturing how they got along without plumbing," Martha said hesitantly. "I'm sure you can carry in water from a well, but what about …"

"They have outhouses," Tim responded, anticipating her question. "And that reminds me of a funny story! Betsy's dad stepped out of their privy one night and stood face to face with a bear. He was lucky; the bear turned and took off. The next day her dad took his tools out back and yanked the door off the outhouse so he could always see what's coming, and from that day on he carried a shotgun with him whenever he headed for the latrine."

"So there was no door for you either!" Martha said laughing.

"Nope. I carried his ol' shotgun too," he said with a wide grin.

"So what happened to you and Betsy?"

Tim looked down and continued in a more serious tone. "That next winter, her dad died. Her mother was talking about moving down to Anchorage to live with her married daughter, but Betsy knew she didn't want to leave the cabin. Betsy decided to quit her job and move into the cabin with her mother at least for a while." He took a sip of his coffee and looked away without meeting Martha's eyes. "She wanted me to go with her, but ..."

"You didn't want to go?"

"Mainly, I didn't want to leave my job on the pipeline, but also the life of an off-gridder was just too tough for me. I like being around people, and I need those modern conveniences we enjoy! I guess I'm spoiled."

Martha thought with a smile that his definition of 'modern conveniences' after a life on America's last frontier was probably much different from hers after a life in Manhattan.

Tim continued, "It was hard telling her I wasn't going with her. We'd been living together in a small apartment on the outskirts of Fairbanks, and I think she felt we'd be making a life together. Something about it just wasn't right though. We were very different people. I wasn't right for her any more than she was right for me."

Martha sat silently as he talked, not sure what to say but knowing it was a difficult story for him to tell.

"I moved back into the barracks and shortly after that I was moved farther south along the pipeline. It just seemed better all around. She stayed on at the cabin, I understand, and eventually married a local guy who knew the ropes better than I did. I'm sure she's doing just fine. She's a tough lady."

Martha liked the kindness in his eyes when he talked about people. He had lived his entire adult life in isolated areas with limited contacts other than the pipeline workers, but he seemed to have developed a deep understanding of people. *He's a good man*, she told herself later that night as she thought about their evening.

As she was falling asleep, it occurred to her that the black car was never around when she was with Tim. *Curious*, she thought as she drifted off.

Chapter 25

"Sarah, I need your help!" The pleading voice coming out of Sarah's answering machine hadn't left a name, but Sarah was sure it was Ruth. She had just returned from taking Barney for a walk. She was cold and took the time to pour a hot cup of coffee before returning the call.

"Hi, Ruth. Are you the person who needs my help?" she asked cheerfully.

"Did I forget to leave my name? I'm sorry. I'm in such a dither!"

"What's going on, Ruth?"

"My application has been approved, and I need to get packed up and ready to leave in three days!"

"Packed up? Leave? Where are you going?"

"Didn't I tell you? I applied to be a vendor at the Midwest quilt show in Chicago. I've been on the waiting list and someone just cancelled. I really don't want to miss this opportunity, but the show starts this Friday!"

"That's exciting, Ruth, but where do I fit in?"

"I want you there with me!"

Sarah had to sit down. This was no time for her to be away, what with Martha's problems. But then, Charles *had* told her to stay out of the investigation, and it looked like being out of town would be the only way she could keep out of it. She and Sophie had already made tentative plans to get involved. She decided she would talk to Sophie and Martha about being away.

"Ruth, give me a couple of hours, and I'll call you with an answer. I'm just not sure. . . ."

"Sarah, please . . . !" Ruth begged. "I really do need you. Anna can't leave the baby, and with Katie in school, I don't have anyone who knows the ropes. Please consider coming with me, all expenses paid and salary to boot! Please?"

"Ruth, I promise I'll give this serious thought. I just have to check out a couple of conflicts. I'll call you before you close the shop this afternoon."

"Okay. I guess that's all I can expect since I'm springing this on you at the last minute. When I didn't hear from them, I just assumed I hadn't been approved. Getting this at the last minute really threw me. Call me later."

Sarah returned the phone to its cradle and sat back down. She thought about how she had changed over the years. When she was younger, it had been easy to change gears, but as the years went by it became harder for her to make quick decisions and sudden changes in her plans.

She was worried about Martha, but Amanda was investigating the stalker and Charles was contacting Greyson's parole officer. *Realistically, what could I be doing for her right now if I stayed in town?* She and Sophie had talked about following Derek for a few days to see if they could catch him in Martha's neighborhood, but Charles had been adamantly opposed to that. And, even if they decided to do it, it didn't need to be done immediately. They could wait to see what Charles and Amanda learned.

Sarah picked up the phone and dialed Sophie. "I need to talk. May I come over?"

"I'll put the kettle on."

Sarah grabbed the leash and surprised a sleeping Barney by immediately hooking it on his collar and announcing, "Let's go, Sleepyhead." Barney stood up and shook, getting his straggly fur relatively presentable. He then realized what was happening and wagged his tail eagerly. They hurried across the street and rang Sophie's doorbell before the kettle had time to whistle.

"How do you like my new doorbell?" Sophie asked as they came in from the cold. "Tim is mighty handy!" she added with a proud smile. "You know, he's talking about retiring and moving back here."

Sarah looked surprised, wondering what affect that would have on Martha. "Soon?" she asked.

"No. But maybe sometime this year."

"That would be wonderful, Sophie. I know you would love having him around."

Ignoring Sarah's comment, Sophie placed two cups of tea on the table and asked, "So what's this big emergency?"

Sarah told her friend about Ruth's dilemma and her own. "I'm just uncomfortable about leaving Martha right now. It was hard for her to tell me about her problems, and it just doesn't seem right for me to turn around and leave town!"

"Stop the dramatics!" Sophie said, waving her hand dismissively. "Martha's a big girl. All you have to do is explain to her that you'll be away for a few days. She'll survive."

"But …"

"No! Just because your girl decided after twenty years to take you into her confidence doesn't mean she is permanently attached to your apron strings. Martha may need your emotional support, but your friend Ruth needs *real* help … help that you know how to give."

"That's true, but …"

"And you can still provide emotional support to your daughter. Call her. Call her every few hours if you need to. Just let her know you care. That's really all she's asking for. She doesn't expect you to solve her problems." Sophie was frowning and got up from the table, turning her back to Sarah.

Sarah was stunned at the intensity of Sophie's response. Usually Sophie was quick to joke about most things, and it surprised her to hear the seriousness in her voice.

"What is it, Sophie? Are you upset with me about something?"

"Not with you," Sophie responded after a short hesitation. "Not with you. It just hurts me to see you missing out on something you want to do when Martha has been so hurtful to you over the years."

"Hurtful? I never thought of Martha as being particularly hurtful. I certainly wasn't happy with her when she practically forced me to sell my home and move here, but I'm glad now because I have a whole new life now." Sarah looked at Sophie and saw that tears were beginning to form in her eyes.

"Sophie. Talk to me! What's going on?"

Sophie sat back down and pulled her apron up to wipe her eyes. "I'm sorry. It's not you, and it's probably not even

Martha that's bothering me. I just see the same thing with Timmy. He's been essentially out of my life for thirty years and here he is back, acting as if nothing ever happened. Over the years, I've cried myself to sleep many nights missing my son and my husband...." Her shoulders began to sag as she hid her face in her hands.

Sarah wanted to say something comforting but knew there was nothing she could say to make it better. Both of their children had gone on with their lives and rightly so. They had been raised to be competent, productive adults, and that's exactly what they were. She laid her hand on Sophie's shoulder and gently rubbed soothingly. "Watching the next generation move on is never easy," she said gently and then added, "but we both know that good parents never hang onto their children just to avoid being left behind."

Sarah wished she could give Sophie a comforting hug but knew how she felt about such displays of affection. "Soppy nonsense," she had often said. To her surprise, Sophie stood and put her arms around Sarah giving her an awkward squeeze. "Thanks for listening," she said softly, but straightening up suddenly adding, "Now where's that chocolate cake?"

After their snack, they continued talking about the logistics of being away: who would take care of Barney, what did she need to take with her, and when would she talk to Charles and Martha. Once the details were worked out, Sarah hurried home to call Ruth.

* * * * *

"Thanks for coming in so early. Let's sit down in the classroom and talk." Sarah and Ruth had agreed to meet before the shop opened on Tuesday to make their plans for the show. "I've never been a vendor at a large show like this. I'm thinking about keeping it small this year, just to learn the ropes. I want to use this show to get acquainted and tell people about our shop, but there'll only be the two of us there. So here's what I'm thinking. As for fabric, I've been thinking about only taking fat quarters and kits. I don't want to get involved with transporting bolts. What do you think?"

"I agree. We have a couple dozen kits already put together. Maybe we should plan to make up more. We have the sample quilts already made for all five of our kits, and they'll make a nice display."

"Good idea!" Ruth responded. "And we have those three Civil War throws. Let's hang those too and take baskets of Civil War fat quarters along with the patterns. Those are all a popular throw size."

"Hmm. Now I'm thinking we should take a few bolts of Civil War fabrics so customers can get their borders as well. Will we have room?"

"If we take Nathan's van and remove the back seat we can do that. I'll call Nathan and see what he thinks." Ruth's husband had always been supportive of her dream to have her own quilt shop and had been instrumental in making that dream possible.

Getting up to pour herself another cup of coffee, Sarah looked contemplative as she said, "Do you think Geoff would be able to print up some fliers or brochures about the online business? It would be good to have something to hand out so people can order additional yardage."

"Good idea! I'll call him next." Geoff was Ruth's brother-in-law, married to her sister Anna. He created the software, and he and Anna ran the online shop out of their home.

Sarah went into the shop and prepared to cut the fabrics for a few kits while Ruth was on the phone. Carefully following the fabric requirements on the patterns, she cut the fabrics that matched the samples, folded them neatly and placed them in plastic bags along with the pattern. She set them aside for Ruth to price. When Ruth finished with the calls, she joined Sarah and they worked together to prepare another twenty-five kits.

"Hi, girls!" Anna hurried into the shop, pulling off her coat as she came through the door. "I'm here to cut fat quarters!" Geoff said you needed me.

"Start with the Civil War collection," Sarah instructed. "We're going to take the five sample quilts that are made with fat quarters, along with the patterns."

"How about the borders?"

"We're talking about taking a dozen or so Civil War bolts, but I'm still thinking about that. Just start with the fat quarters for now, and I have some nice baskets in the back for displaying them."

Although it was always nice to have customers, the three women were pleased that it was a quiet day. At one point, they had so many bolts spread around the shop, they were tripping over them. "I haven't seen this much mess in the shop since our anniversary sale last year!" Anna said giddily.

By 5:00, they were exhausted but agreed that they had made a great start in preparing for the show. They moved everything to an area near the back door and agreed to meet the next day to decide on their next steps.

"Will we be taking your tables?" Sarah asked.

"No. They provide tables and dividers. I told them we need six of each. We'll have four across the back and one on each side. Their tables come with white covers, but let's take a few extra quilts from home to put across the tables as well. And we'll display our samples on the dividers."

"How about displays for equipment and books? Are you taking those from the shop?"

"I have extra wire racks in the back. We'll take those. I don't want the shop to look too empty while we're away."

"We're going to need a cutting board and ruler if we're cutting fabric."

"Hmm. True. And maybe we need an extra table for cutting? I'm having second thoughts about taking yardage. We'll talk about that tomorrow."

"I have an idea," Anna said tentatively. "I was looking at the patterns, and most of them call for two yards of border fabric. Why don't we cut two-yard pieces now instead of cutting fabric at the show? I'm sure we could sell them in the shop if they don't all sell."

"I like that!" Ruth responded. "I think that would make it much simpler since there'll only be the two of us working. Without having to cut, we'll have one person to ring up sales and another to help customers and tell them about our shop."

As they locked the door shivering from the cold evening air, Sarah noted, "I'll bet it's even colder in Chicago!"

Chapter 26

"I'm glad you had time to go out to dinner tonight." Charles held Sarah's chair as she sat and walked around the table to the seat opposite her. They could both watch the glistening snow drifting softly to the ground. Sarah was leaving for Chicago the next morning, and they had returned to the lodge where Charles first broached the topic of marriage.

"I couldn't leave town without seeing you," she responded with a coy smile. "Actually, I wish you were going. You would be a big help to us. ..."

"I could come," he added before she even finished her sentence.

Sarah laughed and explained that she and Ruth had downsized the project and would be able to handle it alone. "We wouldn't have any time together there anyway. I'll be working pretty much nonstop."

"Have you told Martha you're leaving?"

"Yes, and she was fine with it. As she said, there really isn't anything I can do to help right now. Amanda is checking out Derek Kettler, and you're dealing with the Montana folks. And, of course, I'm only going to be gone for the weekend."

"I'll miss you," he said, giving her his *lost puppy* look.

They ordered drinks and an appetizer but decided to hold off on their dinner order. "I have something for you," he said almost reluctantly. "I hope it's not the wrong time...."

"What is it?" she asked curiously.

"Well, you agreed to marry me someday off in the undefined future ..."

"Okay. Enough histrionics!" she said laughing. "What do you have for me?"

He pulled a small velvet box from his jacket pocket and snapped it open. A dainty pink gold engagement ring with a lovely arrangement of delicate diamonds sparkled against the red velvet lining. "Will you be my wife?"

"Of course, I will," she responded with tears in her eyes. "Charles, it's so beautiful. It looks like an antique."

"It is. I found it at an estate sale in Hamilton last year. I hoped that you ..."

"Last year?"

Looking sheepish, Charles dropped his eyes for a moment, then looked up and responded. "Yes, last year. I've hoped for this for a very long time."

Sarah laughed and reached across the table to touch his face. "You are such a good man, Charles Parker! I love you more than you can imagine."

"Does that mean you'll not only marry me far off in the undefined future, but you're willing to wear my ring in the meantime?"

"I will wear your ring forever, you silly, silly man!" He reached across the table and slipped the ring on her finger. It exactly fit.

"It fits!" Sarah exclaimed.

"I know." Then he added quietly, "Martha helped me." They both laughed and awkwardly hugged across the table.

The waiter who had been waiting in the background came toward their table with their drinks. "Congratulations," he said, looking somewhat embarrassed to intrude.

"Thank you," they replied in unison, both wearing Cheshire cat grins.

Chapter 27

"How long will it take us to get there?" Sarah asked, once they got the van packed and were on their way. Charles and Ruth's husband, Nathan, had packed the car for them.

"Chicago is about three hours from here. We should be there by 5:00. We can get checked in and have some dinner before we set up. The room will be available to us from seven until midnight, but I'm hoping to get to bed long before that."

"I agree. The show opens at 9:00, and we'll surely have some finishing touches before the mobs hit the front door."

The drive was uneventful, and the two women were relatively quiet, each lost in her own thoughts. After the first hour, Sarah cleared her throat and casually laid her left hand across the gearshift. Ruth didn't notice at first but then squealed, nearly running the car onto the shoulder. "Sarah! That's an engagement ring!"

Sarah laughed and told Ruth what Charles had said. She already knew they were talking about getting married sometime in the future, but the ring somehow made it seem more real. "I'm so happy for you, Sarah," Ruth said sincerely meaning it. "When do you think you'll set the date?"

Sarah sighed. "I don't know right now, but I told him we'll talk about it when I get back. I guess I shouldn't keep putting him off, but he isn't pressuring me. Maybe sometime next year. Maybe in the spring …" she added barely above a whisper.

She noticed that Ruth seemed to have drifted off into her own thoughts. Sarah had no idea that, at that moment, a wedding quilt was being designed.

* * * * *

Driving home from work, Martha made an important decision. She realized she was allowing herself to be victimized, yet again, by this crazy black car. Feeling empowered after talking to her mother, she decided she was going to confront the driver the next time she saw the car.

She was almost disappointed when she arrived home to find there was no sign of the black car. In fact, her neighborhood looked peaceful and serene when she pulled up in front of her house. The fresh snow was essentially undisturbed, and there were squirrels scampering between the old tree in her front yard and her freshly filled bird feeders. She smiled, feeling that her life was beginning to get on the right track.

As she walked toward her door, a shiny white SUV pulled up to the curb, and a friendly looking man rolled down the window on the passenger side. He leaned across the seat and called to her, "Excuse me, ma'am. Can you tell me how to get to Whippoorwill Court?"

Chapter 28

The Running Stitches vendor's booth looked even better than they had pictured it in their planning sessions. The quilts were pinned to the dividers and below each one were the associated kits and border fabrics. Books were displayed in white racks, and baskets were scattered around on the tables, displaying bundles of fat quarters and assorted patterns. One section was devoted to the Civil War throws and their patterns along with fat quarters displayed by color. Ruth had her wireless tablet that allowed her to process credit cards. The show organizers had provided chairs, but they had little time to sit. A steady progression of quilters came by asking questions, picking up the brochures Geoff had printed, and purchasing kits, patterns, and fat quarters.

In the early afternoon, Sarah took a short break to grab a sandwich and take it up to their room. She called Charles and told him about the show and their sales. When she returned to the table, she encouraged Ruth to take a break and walk through the show. "Good Idea, Sarah. I want to meet some of the other vendors too."

The show was featuring the work of the famous fiber artist, Marsha McIntyre, who lives in Houston and teaches classes to quilters all over the country. When Ruth returned, she excitedly told Sarah that Marsha was planning to have a show at the Quilt Museum in Hamilton the following year. "I think we'll find a way to offer a field trip for our customers. We can rent a bus and go as a group!" Sarah loved seeing Ruth so excited. It had been a difficult winter for her, and this show was just what she needed.

Toward the end of the day, it was becoming obvious that they were going to need more fat quarters and kits since there were two more days of the show and possibly the busiest days, Saturday and Sunday. Ruth called Anna who agreed to start cutting and Ruth's husband, Nathan, said he would drive them up to Chicago the next morning. "Well, Sarah. We're learning!"

They both had trouble sleeping that night from excitement. They talked about the day and decided to start a *show diary* for the next year's planning. They recorded all the things they had done right and the things that needed to be changed for the next show.

Finally, they both fell asleep, and their wake up call seemed to come much too early.

Saturday's show opened with a bang. The crowds huddled around their table asking questions about the Civil War quilts and about the online store. Ruth passed out her business card, making a note on the back, awarding a 25% discount for customers visiting the shop in the next two months. "I want to get some of these folks coming to the shop," she told Sarah later. "Most of these ladies don't live that far from us, and quilters are willing to drive to a nice quilt shop!"

There was no time for a lunch break on Saturday. At one point, Sarah thought she heard her cell phone ringing but didn't get to it in time. Other customers were asking questions, and she forgot about it. An hour later, it rang again. This time she got to it in time and saw that it was Sophie. *Why would Sophie be calling?*

She flipped the phone open and pushed *talk*. "Sophie! What a surprise. I didn't expect to hear from you today. You should see what's going …"

Sophie interrupted saying, "Sarah. Martha has gone missing."

Chapter 29

Sarah ran out of the conference center into the parking lot where she could talk without interruption. She was shaking and felt dazed. "Sophie. Start from the beginning. What's going on and what do you mean *missing*?"

"Tim has been trying to reach her. They had a date scheduled for Thursday night and she didn't answer the door when he arrived to pick her up." Sophie was talking fast and stopped to catch her breath.

"Go on, Sophie," Sarah pleaded, wrapping her arms around her body in an attempt to control the trembling. She was cold, scared, and desperate to know what had happened to her daughter. "Please, Sophie, go on."

"He called her and left a message, but she didn't call back. He called her at work Friday, and they said she hadn't come in and hadn't called. He went back to the house, but still no answer."

Sarah began to cry. "Sophie! Where's my daughter? I need to talk to Charles."

"Wait!" Sophie demanded. "Just wait. Let me tell you the rest. I decided to tell Timmy about Martha's stalker. He was frantic, and we called Charles. Charles called Amanda, and everyone is doing what they can to find her. We have no idea where she might have gone. We were hoping you might know?"

Shaking almost too violently to speak, she responded, "She wouldn't have gone anywhere voluntarily if she had a date with Tim and then work on Friday. Oh, Sophie, what's happened to her? I've got to get home. Let me go see Ruth and …"

"*No!* Stay on the phone, Sarah, until I finish. Nathan is bringing Anna up to Chicago to take your place at the show, and he'll bring you back. They left several hours ago and should be there soon. Go tell Ruth what's happening and pack your bags…. Sarah? Are you still there?"

"Yes," she responded in a faint voice. "Sophie, thank you. You've been …"

"Amanda and Charles will find her, kiddo. Just get home safely." They hung up, and Sarah went to their room to pull herself together before she talked to Ruth. She tried to wash her face and put on lipstick, but her hands were shaking so bad she couldn't control them. She threw her clothes into her suitcase, grabbed her coat, and headed downstairs, trying to control her emotions in the hallway and lobby.

As she approached the Running Stitches booth, she saw Nathan and Anna talking to Ruth. She was relieved to see they were already there. When Ruth saw Sarah, she ran to her and they clung to one another. "It'll be okay," Ruth said repeatedly. "It'll be okay."

Sarah was eager to get back to Middletown and Nathan seemed to sense it. "Are you ready to leave?"

"Yes, please. Let's leave. I want to go home."

* * * * *

Once they were on the road, Sarah began to sob silently into her hands. Nathan reached across the gearshift and patted her arm gently. "I'm so sorry, Sarah, but I truly believe she's okay. Charles and Amanda are doing everything ..."

"I know, Nathan. I know. I'm so sorry to behave this way. I'm just so worried." Sarah was embarrassed to have become so emotional, but she knew Ruth's husband to be a kind and caring man.

"Ruth said you would want to talk to Charles. Would you like to use my cell phone?"

His words pulled her away from her terrifying thoughts and brought her into the present. She immediately knew she had to stop wallowing in her fears and take some positive steps to help her daughter. First of all, she needed to talk to Charles and see what he had discovered. She wiped away her tears and tried to smile.

"Thank you, Nathan. That's exactly what I want to do, but I have my phone." Still shaking, she pulled her cell phone out of her bag and hit the button Charles had set for reaching him.

"I was hoping you'd call," he said as he picked up the phone. "I'm so worried about you. Are you on the road?"

"Yes. Nathan is right here and I'm okay. We left about thirty minutes ago. Tell me what is happening. Have you found her?"

"No, hon. We don't have any leads yet. I've contacted Greyson's parole officer and I'm waiting to hear back from him, and Amanda went to Derek Kettler's apartment but he wasn't home." He didn't tell her that Derek Kettler hasn't been seen for several days. He didn't want to upset her any more than she already was. "We'll find her, sweetheart. I promise." He was immediately sorry he had added his promise. He had a very bad feeling about Martha's disappearance.

Sarah held the phone without speaking. "Are you still there?" he asked after realizing she hadn't spoken.

"Yes," she said simply. "I'm here. I don't feel good about this, Charles. What has happened to my daughter?" Without waiting for his reply, and not really expecting one, she went on to ask what he had learned from Greyson's parole officer. He hesitated a moment but decided he shouldn't be holding back.

"Officer Blackburn said Greyson missed his last appointment." He hesitated when he heard Sarah gasp. "He wasn't concerned about it, he said, because Greyson started a new job, and he probably had trouble getting away. Blackburn's going to the job site today to see him, and he'll call me tonight."

"Okay," she said simply, then added, "I'll see you in a few hours."

"I love you," he responded. "Call me when you get home."

"I will," she replied barely above a whisper. "And I love you, too."

Sarah and Nathan drove for the next hour or so in silence, each lost in their own thoughts. When they were a couple of hours from home, Sarah again picked up her cell phone and dialed her son, Jason.

"Hey, Sarah!" Jennifer answered enthusiastically. "I didn't expect to be hearing from you this weekend. How's the quilt show going?"

"Jenny, something has happened." Her voice cracked and Jennifer's tone immediately changed.

"What?" she responded with alarm. "Are you okay?"

"It's not me, Jenny. It's Martha. We can't find her."

"What do you mean? She's missing?" Jennifer asked sounding confused.

Sarah told her about Tim discovering she wasn't at home or at work. "No one knows where she is," she added and again began to sob.

"Sarah, hold on. There must be an explanation. She's probably just taking the day off," Jenny added dismissively.

"She wouldn't miss her date with Tim nor take off without calling the office. Something has happened to her."

"But …"

"Jenny, you don't know the whole story. Is Jason home?"

"Yes, but …"

"Put him on the other line, and I'll tell both of you what's been going on."

"Mom?" Jason sounded worried. "What's going on? Jenny said Martha's missing?"

Sarah proceeded to tell them about the stalker and about the break-in the previous week. Jason became angry. "Why didn't you tell me?" he demanded. Sarah didn't take his anger seriously. She knew he always became angry when he felt helpless, but it never lasted long. "What can I do?" he asked, already becoming calmer.

"I'm on my way home. I'll call you when I get there. You might call Charles and see if there's anything you can do to help him." She gave the number to her son, and he said he would call right away.

A few minutes later Sophie called to tell her Tim had joined Charles and Amanda and they were retracing Martha's steps. They had talked with the neighbors across the street and on either side of her. "That old lady across the street yelled at my Timmy! She said the police had been there twice already, and she wasn't opening the door again!"

"That's a good sign," Sarah responded. "That means the police are taking this seriously."

"Amanda saw to that!" Sophie then added, "I've got a Crock-Pot stew on. Let me know when you get home, and I'll bring it over."

"I'm not hungry, Sophie...."

"Well, you might not be, but Andy and Caitlyn are waiting for you to get home so they can bring Barney home, and Charles will be there the minute you get home. I certainly intend to come over as well. You'll end up with a houseful of people to feed. You'll be glad to see this Crock-Pot arrive!"

Sarah smiled for the first time in many hours. Her friends were gathering, and she loved them all.

Chapter 30

Nathan pulled up in front of Sarah's house and hopped out of the car, heading for the trunk to get her bag. As they were walking toward the door, Sophie came out of her house and hurried down her walkway. Tim came bursting out behind her hollering, "Wait for me, Mom! You don't have your cane or your coat!" When he caught up with her, he handed her the cane and helped her on with her coat, which was not an easy task since she hadn't stopped hurrying toward Sarah. Sarah met her in the middle of the street and they hugged while Timmy watched somewhat taken aback. He wasn't accustomed to seeing his mother hug anyone.

Turning to him, she simply said, "Deal with it, son. Things change." And she continued on into Sarah's house. "Run on back and get the Crock-Pot," she called to him from Sarah's doorstep. "And bring a couple bottles of wine," she added.

Sarah headed straight for the phone and dialed Amanda's cell phone before she took her coat off. "I didn't have this number with me," she said turning to Sophie.

When Amanda answered, Sarah bombarded her with questions without waiting for answers. "Wait!" Amanda replied laughing. "Give me a chance to speak."

"Sorry. So, what have you found out?"

"Well, for one thing, Derek Kettler is still missing."

"*Missing?*"

"You didn't know!" Amanda exclaimed. "I'm sorry, Sarah. I thought you knew. Yes, we have officers watching the house, but he hasn't been home for at least two days." Amanda caught Sarah up on what had been done. A missing person's report had been filed on Martha and an APB put out for Kettler's car. Martha's neighbors and her co-workers had been questioned, but apparently no one knew or saw anything. Amanda said she would keep Sarah informed.

"Who's this Derek Kettler?" Sophie asked after Sarah was off the phone.

Taking off her coat and boots, Sarah responded, "He's that man that Martha fired a few months ago. He's been rather insistent that she go out with him...."

"Is he the stalker?"

"Who knows. But now he's missing too. That must mean something."

About that time, Charles opened the front door and walked straight for Sarah. She melted into his arms and felt a degree of relief for the first time that day. "What's happening?" she asked after enjoying a moment of comfort.

"Amanda was able to get a search warrant for Martha's house. She and a couple of officers are going over to see if they can find any evidence of what might have happened. They've already searched outside."

"Did they find anything?"

"Well, it's questionable. It snowed several days ago so there are lots footprints. There's this one set that appears to go part way up the walk toward the house and then it stops. Unfortunately, there are big boot prints that obliterate part of that set which they think are the mail carrier's prints. Those go right up to the mailbox and back. But those first ones are small, like a woman's."

"They only go part way up the walkway?" Sarah asked confused.

"Yes, and then they appear to turn around and take a few steps. Then perhaps there was a struggle...."

Sarah gasped and covered her mouth with the back of her hand. "Martha?"

"We don't know that," Charles said pulling her into his arms again. "Like I said, the snow's a mess out there. There are many prints in the snow, and most of them are smudged. Let's just wait for the official investigation," he added trying to reassure her.

Sophie pulled a pile of bowls out of the cupboard and placed them by the Crock-Pot along with silverware and a loaf of sliced Italian bread. "Help yourselves to food in the kitchen," she announced. Tim filled a bowl and sat down at the kitchen table. Charles filled a bowl and brought it to Sarah in the living room where she was sitting on the couch.

"I'm not really hungry," she said, giving him an apologetic look.

"Just a few bites, okay? You haven't eaten all day."

"I want to go by Martha's house. Can we do that?"

Charles hesitated and then responded, "Let's wait awhile and give Amanda and her people time to check out the house. We can't go in while they're there. In fact, I'll call and ask her to give us a call when you can go in." He handed her the bowl and a fork and turned to leave before she had a chance to refuse the food. The next time he looked, she was taking a tentative bite. He smiled and turned to Sophie, giving her shoulders a quick squeeze. "Thanks for bringing the food over. Our gal needed nourishment."

Sophie turned to Timothy and said, "When you finish eating, hop on over to the house and get those pies. They're in the warming oven." Later as he was leaving, she added, "And bring that gallon of ice cream along, too."

A couple of hours later, Amanda called and said they were just about finished. Sarah and Charles bundled up and hurried out to his car. The temperature was rapidly dropping and a major front was rolling in, bringing with it snow and icy conditions.

By the time they arrived at Martha's house, one squad car was pulling away from the curb, and Amanda had just turned to lock the door. They started to get out, but Amanda motioned for them to wait and headed for their car. She opened the door and slid into the backseat. "Let's talk here since your car is all warmed up."

"Did you find anything?" Charles asked eagerly.

"Nothing. My guess is that the house is just as she left it when she went to work Thursday. I don't think she made it home Thursday night. At least, not into the house."

"What do you mean?" Sarah asked, turning so she could see Amanda's face as she talked.

"There's evidence of a struggle near the curb just in front of her car. We can't be sure it's Martha, but odds are that it is."

Sarah collapsed against Charles and began sobbing uncontrollably. After a moment, Amanda added, "I'm sorry, Sarah. I know this is hard on you." Turning to Charles, she added, "I think you should take her home and stay there. I'll call if we come up with anything."

"Maybe I should be home," Sarah said through her tears. "Maybe Martha will try to call me. ..."

"Good thought! You go on home. I'll talk to you later." Amanda slipped out of the car and headed for her squad car.

Charles pulled away from the curb just as Sarah spoke. "I shouldn't have gone away. This is all my fault."

"What? This isn't your fault, Sarah. In no way is it your fault!"

"I knew about her troubles. I should have taken her to my house where she would be safe, and I should have stayed with her."

"Sarah. Sarah. Sweetheart." He pulled over to the curb and turned to pull her into his arms. "This isn't your fault. Whatever happened was going to happen whether you were at home or in Chicago. And she's a grown woman. Do you really think you could have talked her into moving into your house?"

Sarah smiled meekly through her tears. "I guess not."

Just as they pulled up in front of Sarah's house, Charles cell phone rang. He answered it and turned to Sarah indicating she should go on in. When she opened the front door, she was greeted by a galloping dog who couldn't control himself well enough to resist jumping up on her. Fortunately Tim was standing nearby and was able to steady her so she didn't fall backwards. "Barney! You know better!" She tried to sound harsh but was so glad to see her furry friend that she couldn't fuss at him."

"That dog's a walking disaster," Sophie hollered from the kitchen. "Get in here, Barney," she demanded.

Barney turned and ran into the kitchen, knowing full well that Sophie had a special treat for him. He looked into his bowl and found it filled with warm beef stew. He looked at her with love before the slurping began.

"When did Barney get home?" Sarah asked as she hung up her coat.

"Andy and Caitlyn brought him over a few minutes ago. They didn't think they should stay, but Andy asked that we call them when we hear something.

"Was he good for them while I was away?" Sarah asked.

"Humph," Sophie responded.

Charles came in quietly and sat down at the table. Tim had gone home and only the three friends remained. Sarah poured three cups of coffee, and she and Sophie joined him at the table. "What was the call?" Sarah asked, knowing whatever it was had disturbed him.

"It was Blackburn in Montana."

"Who's Blackburn?" Sophie asked.

"Greyson's parole officer," Sarah responded. Turning to Charles, she asked timidly not really wanting to hear his answer, "What did he have to say?"

"Greyson has violated his parole. He's left town."

Chapter 31

The next morning, Sarah got out of bed after a long night of tossing and turning. She had dozed occasionally but had immediately awakened from terrifying dreams. She was exhausted and her head throbbed. She took a long hot shower, a couple of aspirin, and was beginning to feel somewhat better when the phone rang.

"Hi, sweetie. How are you doing this morning?"

"Better now," she responded. "Has anything happened?"

"Not a thing," Charles responded. "I called Amanda this morning, but I got the machine. She probably worked most of the night and is getting some sleep. I left a message. So, may I come over?"

"Of course! I'm getting ready to make some breakfast. Have you eaten?" she asked as cheerfully as she could manage.

"Not yet. Just put the coffee on, and I'll come make breakfast for us. I'm bringing country bacon. Do you have eggs?"

Sarah felt her stomach tighten at the thought of a big breakfast, but she knew she needed to eat. She had a tendency to lose her appetite when she was stressed but knew it was important for her to eat. She started the coffee and took milk and butter out of the refrigerator. After turning the oven on, she reached for the flour, baking powder, and a large mixing bowl and began making biscuits. Cooking always settled her down when she was feeling at loose ends.

As she was placing the carefully formed biscuits on the baking sheet, she heard Charles' car pull up. Barney heard it too and rushed to the front door, getting there well ahead of Sarah. "Barney, you've been forgetting your manners. When Charles comes in, *do not* jump up on him!" Her words carried a touch of harshness and Barney's ears and tail drooped despondently. Sarah was immediately sorry, knowing that he didn't understand her words. She held his collar and gently directed him to sit, which he did obediently. "Stay." She added as she opened the door for Charles. Barney trembled with excitement but held the position until Sarah said, "Okay!"

Charles, knowing what was going on, quickly knelt down to Barney's level, and they greeted one another in their usual boisterous manner, both tumbling onto the floor in a jovial tussle. Fortunately, Sarah had grabbed the grocery bag just in time to save it from being destroyed by the horseplay.

"You two silly boys!" Sarah said as she headed for the kitchen where she opened the package of bacon and took a skillet out of the cabinet.

"Stop!" Charles said as he entered the kitchen. "That's my job!" He reached into the refrigerator, removed a carton of eggs, and moved to the stovetop. Sarah slipped the biscuits into the preheated oven and sat down with her coffee to watch as Charles prepared breakfast for the two of them.

Knowing she was watching him, he turned and winked. Her love for him felt almost overwhelming.

"Thank you," she said gently.

"For breakfast? This is nothing special. ..."

"Not just for breakfast. For caring about my daughter and for being there for me and for being such a special man! Thank you for all that and much more."

Charles slipped the skillet off the fire and turned to her. His eyes were moist as he looked down at her. Wordlessly, he pulled her into his arms and held her close. She felt the tension drain from her body and her mind. It was suddenly clear to her that all her years of fighting for her independence were foolish.

People are not meant to be alone, she thought as she sighed deeply and melted into the warmth of his arms.

* * * * *

Charles and Sarah decided to spend the day together. Amanda was going to stop by later to let them know what progress had been made, and Charles was waiting to hear from Officer Blackburn regarding their progress in finding out where Greyson had gone. When Sarah suggested they bundle up and take Barney for a walk, he slipped his cell phone into his pocket after making a quick call to Amanda to let her know where they would be and asking her to call him when she was on her way.

"Maybe I shouldn't go. Maybe I should stay by the phone in case Martha calls," Sarah said as they were starting out the door. The tension was returning to her face.

"Does she know your cell phone number?"

"Yes. Good point! She'll call my cell if I'm not home. Wait while I run in and get it." She handed Barney's leash to Charles and turned to go back in just as the phone rang. The readout said "private caller" and when Sarah answered, she heard the caller disconnect. Charles had returned to the foyer with a hesitant Barney and asked her who was on the phone.

"No one," she responded, looking worried. "They hung up." After the disturbing call, Sarah was again reluctant to go out, but Charles convinced her it would be fine. He knew that the fresh air and exercise would help her.

They walked slowly toward the dog park with his arm around her shoulder and leaving their tracks in the freshly fallen snow. As they approached the park, Barney began to pull against the leash and whine. Once inside the gate, Sarah snapped the leash off and let him run. He headed straight for a low-growing juniper. His tail was swishing back and forth wildly, and his whine had grown in intensity. Once he was close to the bush, he began to bark a sharp, insistent bark. He ran back and forth between the bush and Sarah, barking and whining. Sarah hurried to the bush to see what was upsetting him.

"I think he's trying to tell us that Timmy has fallen in the well," Charles joked as he walked toward them.

Sarah laughed but then remarked, "You aren't far off! Come see what's in the bush."

Charles caught up with them and bent to see what was there. Deep inside the branches lay a small kitten. He appeared to be no more than a few weeks old. His eyes were open, and he was mewing ferociously for such a small creature. Barney pushed through his family, trying desperately to get to the kitten. At this point, he had stopped barking but continued to whine. Charles reached in, picked the kitten up, and slipped him inside his coat where it was warm. "He's freezing!" The kitten immediately began to purr, perhaps understanding that his struggles were coming to an end.

"How do you suppose he got here?" Sarah asked, reaching into Charles' coat and tucking the end of his scarf around the kitten. "Where do you think the mother is?" She looked around, but there was no sign of cats or even prints in the snow. "He must have been here since before this last snowfall. There are no prints leading to the bush.

"He's lucky to be alive," Charles commented, "in this cold. Let's get him home and feed him. Do you have milk?"

"I have milk, but I'll call Barney's vet and find out what the little guy should be eating. Let's hurry home. He's very cold." Barney seemed to accept the fact that the kitten was safe inside Charles' coat. At first, he jumped up trying to get to him, but Charles leaned down and let Barney look inside and see that the kitten was okay. The three, now four, hurried home. While Charles wrapped the kitten in a warm afghan and continued to hold him close, Sarah called Doctor Brian, the veterinarian who had helped her when she first brought Barney home from the kennel.

After a few minutes, Sarah took the bundle from Charles and asked him to warm up the car. "The doctor wants to see him right away." As they were dressing to leave again, Barney became very agitated. He paced back and forth, whining and occasionally barking a low concerned bark. "I think we should take Barney with us." Sarah said. "He's too worried to be left here alone."

"Okay. I'll take him with me and we'll get the car warmed up for you two." When Charles came back for Sarah and the kitten, she was ready to go. "How's the little guy doing?" he asked.

"He seems content, but I'm worried about him. He's become very lethargic." Together they hurried to the car. Barney was ensconced in the backseat and Sarah, with her bundle, slipped into the front. Barney took one look over the seat to make sure everything was okay and settled back down on the back seat.

As they drove, Sarah reached into her pocket and wrapped her fingers around her cell phone as if it brought her closer to her daughter. She wished that Martha would call. She hoped that Martha was *able* to call. Despite the distraction caused by the helpless kitten, unspoken prayers for her daughter's safety continued to occupy her every thought.

Doctor Brian Mayfield's office was an easy ten-minute drive from Sarah's house. When they arrived, the receptionist was expecting them and took them back to an examining room. Charles brought a worried Barney along, assuring him the visit was not for him.

"This is one lucky kitten," the doctor announced after a careful examination. "You found her just in time."

"Her?" Sarah responded with surprise. "I don't know why we assumed it was a male. Is she okay?"

"She'll be just fine once we get her hydrated and some nourishment in her. She couldn't have been out there very long or she wouldn't have survived in these temperatures. Do you have any idea where she came from?"

"None," they responded in unison.

"Hmm. She's probably a feral that got separated from her mother. She's just lucky you found her when you did."

"Actually, Barney found her. She was under a bush in the dog park."

Looking at Barney, the doctor replied, "Good work, boy!" Barney smiled and wagged his tail. "Are you going to keep her?" the doctor asked, turning to Sarah.

"Of course!" she responded, looking at Charles who was nodding his agreement.

As they watched the doctor complete his examine, it was the first time they were able to get a good look at the tiny kitten. The doctor told them she was about three weeks old. Her long, disheveled fur was black with a small amount of white sprinkled throughout. She had snow-white paws and a white bib on her chest that reached around her neck like an elegant fur necklace. Her eyes were light blue, but the doctor said they would change, most likely to yellow or copper.

Doctor Brian then set up her shot schedule and sent his assistant, Stephanie, in to teach the new family how to feed their kitten.

"What's this little girl's name?" Stephanie asked after she fed her and handed the box of formula to Charles.

"We found her just a few hours ago and haven't had a chance to think about it," Sarah responded. Looking at Charles she asked, "Any suggestions?"

"Well, maybe we need to give it some thought, but looking at her little white paws, I'm inclined to say maybe Boots or Socks. What do you think?"

Sarah tilted her head and studied the kitten more closely. "She sort of looks like a Boots or maybe a Bootsy?" she said questioningly. "Bootsy?" she repeated looking at the kitten. The kitten turned her head toward Sarah and mewed softly.

"I think she likes it," Stephanie said, picking up the kitten and handing her to Sarah.

Sarah nestled her face into the tiny kitten's fur and said, "So Bootsy it is." Little Bootsy licked Sarah's chin with her tiny pink tongue and began purring.

"With a full tummy, the kitten slept all the way home curled up inside Sarah's coat. They stopped at the drug store so Charles could get kitty litter and a heating pad. The doctor told them she should sleep with it set on the lowest setting. Once they got home, Sarah retrieved a shoebox and asked Charles to cut a hole so Bootsy could get in and out. They then filled it with batting scraps and set it on the heating pad. They decided to put the box in Sarah's bedroom next to Barney's bed so he could look in on her during the night.

Barney, who had been pacing and whining since they got home, finally settled down once the kitten was curled up in her box. "As soon as we find Martha, I'll make Bootsy a quilt," Sarah said with a smile, watching the tiny ball of fur as she snuggled down into the warm bedding. Turning to leave, she said, "Come on, Barney. She's fine now." Instead of following Sarah and Charles to the kitchen, Barney got into his own bed, circled three times and laid down with his head facing the shoebox. He sighed deeply and closed his eyes.

"He's gone to bed!" Sarah exclaimed. "It's three in the afternoon and he's gone to bed! He always takes his afternoon naps on his mat in the kitchen."

"I guess things will be different now that there's a baby in the house," Charles replied with a chuckle.

Chapter 32

The next morning Sarah got up early, eager to check on the kitten. She had been up several times during the night taking her to the litter box and giving her warmed formula. The little fur ball was becoming more active and purred while she ate.

Looking into the box, Sarah didn't see the kitten right away but assumed she was nestled into her bedding. She pulled the batting aside and was disturbed to find that the box was empty.

"Where's the kitten?" she asked Barney, not expecting an answer. Barney opened his eyes but didn't move. Sarah came closer and saw the kitten curled up against Barney's chest. She was barely visible as Barney had covered her protectively with his paw. Sarah carefully lifted Bootsy out of the warm nest Barney had provided and carried her into the kitchen with Barney following right behind, keeping a possessive eye on his new charge.

Sarah decided to spread a quilt out on the floor, so they could both stay in the kitchen during the day. She put the heating pad under the quilt and laid the kitten on it after feeding her and reminding her where the litter box was located. Barney, of course, very carefully laid down on the quilt and wrapped his body around her, sighing deeply.

"You are going to make a good daddy," Sarah assured him, handing him one of his favorite treats and patting his head.

The previous night, Greyson's parole officer had called Charles to say there was still no news on Greyson's whereabouts. "It must be him," Sarah overheard Charles say to the caller, but he hadn't repeated it to Sarah when he got off the phone.

As she sat thinking about her daughter, the phone rang and Sarah felt her stomach tighten. She hoped for good news yet feared the worst. Despite her trepidation, she hurried to answer the phone.

"Amanda! I'm so glad you called. Is there any news?"

"Nothing very helpful, Sarah, I'm sorry to say. Charles and I were speculating that Greyson was probably involved in this, but now we've learned that Derek Kettler still hasn't been located. He hasn't been home for several days, and none of the neighbors know anything about him.

"Does he have family?"

"We checked with Martha's company since he used to work there. They had an emergency number listed, but it's been disconnected. We found out it belonged to a man with the same last name, Kettler. Maybe a brother, maybe not. Anyway, we haven't been able to locate him either."

"Do you have any other leads?" Sarah asked, afraid they were at a standstill.

"None, Sarah, I'm sorry to say. I contacted Martha's company but didn't get anywhere. They're so concerned with security that they are totally closed to outsiders, even the police. I spoke with the head of Human Resources once and with Martha's supervisor a couple of times, but neither had any information they are willing to share. I asked if they thought her disappearance could be related to their internal investigation, and they wouldn't even admit there *was* an investigation!"

"I'm wondering if Alan would help us."

"Alan?"

"Alan is the man Martha hired to replace Derek. I don't know his last name, but I might be able to get through to him through Martha's secretary. I met her once. I think I'll give that a try. He might know something."

"I hesitate for you to get involved in the investigation, Sarah. It could be dangerous. On the other hand, they aren't going to talk to me, and they just might talk to you. Go ahead and give it a try but be careful."

After they hung up, Sarah finally got around to making coffee and pouring a bowl of cereal. Bootsy and Barney were sleeping soundly on the heating pad, looking very content. "That kitten has landed in the lap of luxury," Sarah said aloud. Barney opened one eye and looked at her, wagged his tail once, and nestled in closer to the kitty.

Sitting at the kitchen table sipping her coffee, Sarah racked her brain trying to remember the name of Martha's secretary. Over the last few years, it was becoming harder to remember things, particularly names. At first, this worried her, but one day she read an article about dementia and felt reassured to learn that forgetfulness was a normal and expected part of growing older.

She had developed a habit of associating a picture with a name as a way of remembering. The vision of sap running down the side of a tree, or *running tree sap*, was her way of remembering the name of one of her favorite country music singers, Ronnie Milsap!

Stopping to think about Martha's office, she resurrected a mental picture of an imaginary shell sitting on the edge of the secretary's desk. *Shell?* She thought curiously. Then, "Shelly? No! *Sheila!*" she said aloud with a smile. She hurried to the phone and dialed Martha's office.

"Martha Miller's office."

"May I speak with Sheila, please?"

"This is she. How can I help you?"

"Sheila, this is Sarah Miller. I'm Martha's mother. ..."

"Oh, Mrs. Miller! I'm so sorry to hear about Martha. Has there been any word?"

"Nothing," she responded, trying to keep her voice from cracking. "I was wondering if you could help me with something."

"Of course! Anything."

"Martha often mentioned a man who works in your office by the name of Alan. I was wondering if you could give me his name and tell me how to reach him." The line fell quiet, and Sarah wondered if they had been disconnected. "Hello?"

"I'm sorry, Mrs. Miller. Yes, of course, I can help. His name is Alan Fitzgerald, but I don't think he's involved. ..."

"Oh no, Sheila! I don't think he's involved either. I just want to talk with him. He might know something that he doesn't even realize is important." The two women continued to talk for a few minutes, and Sarah jotted down the number Sheila gave her.

The kitten stretched and let out a loud, somewhat demanding meow. Barney was instantly alert, and Sarah hurried over and took her to the litter box. This time she didn't carry her but helped her move in the right direction. Once Bootsy got close, she recognized it and hopped right in. Her little scratches caused litter to fly out of the box, hitting Barney on the nose. He shook his head violently while Sarah laughed at the two of them. Once the mess was swept up, she sent a very reluctant Barney out the back door and held the kitten in her lap while she finished her coffee. A half-hour later, both of her furry creatures were curled up together on the quilt.

She sat down to dial Alan Fitzgerald's number.

"Fitzgerald," he answered, sounding somewhat distracted.

"Mr. Fitzgerald. I'm Sarah Miller, Martha's mother, I'm calling …"

"Mrs. Miller! I'm so glad you called. What's happening? Have they found her?" He sounded very concerned and eager to hear good news.

As hard as it was to keep telling the story repeatedly, she filled him in on most of what had been done to locate her. She didn't mention the disappearance of Greyson or of Kettler. She didn't want to tell too much. Martha had expressed some misgivings regarding Alan, although she seemed to trust him.

"How can I help?" he finally asked after she told him as much as she was willing to share.

"Something has been troubling me. I can't help but think that it might be more than coincidence that Martha has disappeared right at the time that something shady seems to be going on at the lab. I'm actually wondering …"

"Let's not talk about this on the phone," Alan said, interrupting Sarah. "I'll come right over. Where are you?"

Sarah gave Alan her address, and he said he would be there within the hour. She realized she hadn't taken the time to shower or dress, so she hurried to her room. She started to call Charles first, but decided she wanted to have the conversation with Alan alone. She hoped that wasn't a mistake.

Over an hour later, Alan still hadn't arrived, and Barney was eager for his walk. She tucked the kitten into her box in the bedroom and snapped Barney's leash on, telling him they were going for a walk. He didn't exhibit his usual enthusiasm and kept looking back toward her bedroom door. "Bootsy will be fine! Let's take a short walk." She stayed on their street so she could see if a car pulled up in front of her house.

Ten minutes later, a black car turned the corner and pulled up to the curb. As Sarah approached the car, she could see part of the license plate. The remainder was smudged, perhaps by mud. The first letters were *E6*. Sarah stood frozen in place, remembering the black car that was following her daughter as she left the shop. It was the same car! She remembered Martha telling her that Amanda had checked for those limited numbers but was unable to come up with a match. She felt the blood drain from her head. She was immobilized, not knowing what to do.

But her anger and her desperation won out. She dropped the leash and ran up to him, beating his chest with her fists. "Where is she? What have you done with my daughter?" she demanded through angry tears.

Barney was now loose and ran up as well, unsure what to do. He began to growl and pull at Alan's pant leg.

"What's going on here?" Alan demanded, grabbing Sarah's wrists. "Stop hitting me! Please! Calm down and tell me what's wrong."

"Your car! It was you!"

"*What* was me? I don't know what you're talking about." Although he could have easily been angry by Sarah's attack, he seemed instead to be bewildered and confused.

Jerking loose from his hands, she said, "You're the one who's been stalking my daughter. I know this car!"

"Mrs. Miller. Sarah. Please. First of all, this is *not* my car. My Acura is in the shop. I'm driving my wife's car. ..."

The blood drained from Sarah's face as she stared at Alan. "Your wife's car?" she repeated. "Your *wife's* car?"

"Yes, my wife's car. What's going on here?"

She didn't know if she could trust him, but she was desperate to find out about her daughter. Charles' and Amanda's words echoed in her mind. *Stay out of the investigation. Leave it to the professionals.* Turning to Alan and dismissing their warnings, she said, "We need to talk."

The two strangers who had so recently been in a physical altercation out on the street were now sitting around the kitchen table, sipping coffee and comparing notes. Charles had joined them, as had Amanda.

"Okay," Amanda said, looking first at Alan, then at Sarah. "Start from the beginning."

Sarah had already told Alan about the stalker and was surprised to learn that he knew nothing about it. "Martha never even let on," he said. Charles, originally very suspicious of him, had decided he was telling the truth.

Alan shared with the group that his wife, Jillian, had been plagued with emotional problems since the birth of their last baby and was insanely jealous of Martha. "We spend a lot of time working together, and Jillian just can't accept that it's strictly a professional relationship."

"Is she violent?" Amanda asked. Sarah shuddered.

Alan hesitated. "She has been. But only with me. I don't think she would hurt anyone else. Wait!" he demanded abruptly, looking at Amanda. "Are you thinking she did something to Martha?"

"I would like to talk to her about that," Amanda responded.

"No. It wasn't Jillian," he insisted. "I'm sure of it. She's been home all week and in a good mood. She hasn't even mentioned …" but then he hesitated.

"She doesn't seem to be as worried about …" again he stopped. Turning to Amanda, he said, "Give me time to talk to her. I know we can straighten this out." He stood and pulled his cell phone out of his pocket. Amanda stood and told him to put the phone down.

"What?"

"I don't want you to warn her. I want to go talk to her now. You can go with me."

Charles and Sarah stood as well. "We want to go to."

"I don't think …" Amanda began, but saw the desperation in Sarah's eyes and didn't finish. "Okay, follow me. Mr. Fitzgerald, I want you to ride in the squad car with me."

Sarah quickly moved the kitten's bed into the kitchen next to the litter box and pulled her coat back on. Barney looked confused, but Sarah had more important things on her mind right then.

"Take care of the baby," she said to him as she hurried out the door.

Chapter 33

A lan, sitting in the back seat of the squad car, directed Amanda to his home. Charles and Sarah followed close behind. When they arrived, a second squad car pulled up with his siren on. Amanda frowned. "That's my partner. I should have told him to come in quietly."

A woman in her mid-thirties opened the front door and came rushing out. Her hair was disheveled and she was dressed in jeans and a flannel shirt. She wrapped her arms around her body in an attempt to stave off the bitter cold. "What's going on?" she yelled in anger. Her fiery eyes scanned past Sarah, Charles, and the police officers and settled on Alan. "What have you done now?" she shouted, glaring at him. "And where have you been?"

"Calm down, Jillie. These police officers want to ask you a few questions."

Sarah started toward her, but Charles held her back. "Let Amanda and her partner handle this, hon. They know what they're doing."

"But Martha ..." she started to object, but stopped.

"I know," he said gently. "Just stay back here with me and Amanda will find out if this woman is involved.

Amanda stepped forward and introduced herself and her partner. "Are you Jillian Fitzpatrick?"

"Yes," the woman responded, her black eyes shooting daggers at the strangers in her yard.

"May we go inside and talk?"

"What's this about?"

"May we go inside?" Amanda repeated.

The woman hesitated, then dropped her eyes and nodded half-heartedly. "Go on." On her way in, she turned to Amanda and angrily said, "Who are these people?"

Once they were inside, Amanda introduced Sarah and Charles and explained that Sarah was the mother of a woman who has gone missing. "So?" Jillian responded. "What's that to me?"

"We think you might have information that would help us locate the woman."

"Me? I know nothing about a missing woman. ..."

"Do you drive a black 1998 Ford Escort, license E6-WRT-78?"

"I drive an old Ford, sure. But I have no idea what the license plate says. Why?" she demanded impatiently.

Amanda had already confirmed that Jillian Fitzpatrick was the registered owner of the car sitting outside Sarah's house but was simply testing the woman's reaction to being questioned about the car.

"What's all this about my car? Alan? Where's the car?" She then started screaming at him again, "What have you done to my car?"

"Calm down, Mrs. Fitzpatrick," Amanda responding, stepping between Alan and his wife. "Your car is fine. We have a few questions for you. The woman who is missing lives on South Sycamore and your car has been seen in that area during the past few weeks."

"So? It's a free world. I can drive anywhere I want," Jillian responded defensively. "I haven't done anything wrong," she added, glancing at Alan for confirmation.

"That's true, Mrs. Fitzpatrick. As far as we know, you haven't done anything wrong. However, you might have seen something while you were driving in that neighborhood. The woman who is missing is Martha Miller. She …"

"She's missing?" Jillian responded with astonishment. "When?" she asked apprehensively.

"She hasn't been seen since Thursday afternoon," Sarah announced. She didn't mean to interfere with the investigation, but the questioning was going much too slowly. Her patience was growing thin. She wanted to find Martha *now*.

Amanda looked at Sarah disapprovingly. Charles laid his hand on her arm and gently guided her back down onto the couch. Sarah mumbled, "Sorry."

Turning to Jillian, Amanda asked, "Were you driving on Sycamore Thursday afternoon?" She had the words out before she realized that Jillian appeared to be in shock. All the color had drained from her face and she was covering her mouth with her hands.

"Oh no," Jillian muttered. "No!"

"What is it, Mrs. Fitzgerald?"

Jillian had trouble forming her words. Alan realized she was trembling and moved to her side. He placed his arm around her shoulder, and said gently, "What it is, Jillie?"

"I saw it. I saw him take her."

* * * * *

After listening to Jillian's story, Amanda suggested they move to the station house to continue the interrogation. She walked Jillian to her squad car and asked her partner to transport Alan separately. Amanda was still concerned about keeping them apart so that Alan couldn't influence what Jillian might add to her story.

"I didn't know," Jillian wailed over and over as Amanda walked her to the squad car. "I didn't know."

Driving toward the station with Jillian securely in the back seat, Amanda thought about what had transpired during the last half hour at the Fitzgerald house. Through near hysterical tears, Jillian had managed to tell the group that she saw a man in a white SUV pull up and call out to Martha. She said that Martha had just arrived home and turned to respond to the man.

According to Jillian, Martha walked over to the passenger's side of the car and they spoke briefly. Suddenly the man opened the door and attempted to pull her inside. Martha seemed to be resisting when suddenly the man jumped out of the car and forced her into the backseat.

"Then they drove away," she had said, "I wondered if I should do something. ..."

Listening to Jillian's story, Sarah had become very upset and angrily reproached the woman saying, "Why didn't you call the police?" Both Sarah and Jillian became inconsolable. It was at that time that Amanda decided to move her investigation to the police station with its various interview rooms and technology.

Sarah had pleaded with Amanda to allow her to go as well, but Amanda refused. She asked Charles to take Sarah home, and she promised to call the minute she had any useful information. Charles wanted to go to the station as well but knew his place was with Sarah.

As Amanda approached the station, she realized that her passenger had become very quiet. She looked back and saw that Jillian was just staring ahead. There was no emotion on her face at all.

Later, as Amanda was helping her out of the squad car, Jillian appeared limp and was hardly able to stand. An empty pill bottle rolled off her lap and landed in the gutter next to the car.

Chapter 34

Charles arrived at Sarah's house early the next morning, knowing she was eagerly awaiting a call from Amanda. When the phone finally rang, she and Charles rushed to it simultaneously. Charles stepped back and motioned for Sarah to answer. It was Amanda and she asked for Charles without offering any other information. Sarah passed the phone to Charles but was frantic to know what was going on. As he answered, she reached across him and tapped the speaker button so she could listen.

"Charles, I need your help."

"I'll help in any way I can, Amanda, but what's going on?"

"First of all, Jillian Fitzgerald is in the hospital."

"What?" Sarah cried from the background. "What happened to her?"

"Am I on speaker?" Amanda asked.

"Yes, Amanda. Sarah is desperate to know what's going on. Just go ahead."

"Okay. Well, she managed to ingest pills on the way to the station house last night. I don't know how many yet. The prescription bottle was in her purse. It had been filled almost a month ago, so we're hoping there weren't that many pills left."

"When will you be able to talk to her?" Charles asked.

"I'm on my way to the hospital now."

Sarah moved closer to the phone and spoke. "Has she said anything else about Martha?"

"Not yet. But there's been a development."

"What?" Sarah hollered.

Charles frowned and said, "Please, hon. Let me talk." Then, into the phone he asked, "What's going on, Amanda? Sarah is beside herself with worry."

"Once the EMT left with Mrs. Fitzgerald, the desk sergeant gave me a message. Derek Kettler had been brought in for questioning and was waiting in an interview room."

"Yes?" Charles responded eagerly. "What did he have to say? Does he have Martha?" Sarah gripped his arm so tightly, he thought she would cut off circulation to his hand.

"He's been out of town. We confirmed that he was in Kentucky visiting his brother. He went there on Tuesday of last week and arrived back here late last night."

"Are you sure? Maybe he …"

"It wasn't him, Charles."

"You said you need my help. What can I do?"

"The possibilities are shrinking. I spent several hours with Alan last night, and we both feel there is no chance that the mole in their lab had anything to do with Martha's disappearance. According to Alan, there's no way Martha could be of any help to them. They already have the test results. There's just no reason for them to kidnap her. And if, by any chance, she's being held as a hostage, we would have heard from her captors by now."

Sarah gasped. "Hostage?" She became pale and looked as if she were about to faint.

"Hold on!" Charles said, dropping the phone and leading Sarah to a chair. "Sarah, she said that is *not* likely. That is *not* what they are thinking happened. Now rest here and let me find out what Amanda wants me to do."

Sarah nodded weakly. "Okay. I'm sorry."

He kissed her cheek and returned to the phone, taking it off speaker. "Okay, what can I do to help?"

"As I was saying, the pool of possible perpetrators is shrinking. My money is on that Greyson guy, and you have a relationship with his parole officer. How do they know he left town? Where was he headed? How was he traveling? Does he have a white SUV? I could call and talk to him or even go through the local precinct there, but I think you can get to the bottom line much faster than I can. Would you call him and see what you can find out?"

"I'll get right on it."

They talked a few more minutes about the case and hung up. Charles turned to Sarah who was still sitting where he had placed her. "What did she want you to do?" she asked but seemed somewhat withdrawn.

"What is it?" he asked, responding to her demeanor rather than her question.

"I'm okay. I guess I was upset that you were treating me like an out-of-control child," she said, but smiled weakly and added, "but I guess that's how I was acting. I'm just so worried...."

"I know, sweetheart. I know. I'm sorry about the way I responded. Taking over and issuing commands is second nature to me, but I promise to try to do better. You know I love you."

"I know," she responded with a timid smile. "I know. So what does she want you to do?"

He told her everything Amanda had said, wishing he had just left the speaker button on.

"Let's get a cup of coffee first," he suggested. "It's still early in Montana." Sitting in the kitchen, he pulled out the notebook he had started carrying in his chest pocket. The pad had been a part of him for the thirty years he was in the department, but he had been trying to break the habit since he retired. Right now, he needed it. He jotted down the questions Amanda wanted answered and a couple of his own.

Sarah scooped a large helping of her freshly cooked oatmeal into a bowl for Charles and topped it with blueberries and milk. She picked up the kitten and held it on her lap while she had her coffee and attempted to make light conversation while he ate.

An hour or so later, Charles stood and announced, "I think it's late enough to call him."

"Would you talk from the kitchen so I can at least hear your side of the conversation?"

"Of course," he responded standing to give her a hug and retrieve the phone.

Sarah took advantage of the time to carry Bootsy to the litter box. "But when you finish on the phone, we need to get Barney out of this house. He's been curled up in his bed for several days now!"

She heard Charles' chuckle from the other room.

Walking back into the kitchen, Charles had his cell phone clipped to his shirt pocket and a wire running to this ear. Sarah looked at him inquisitively, and he responded with a coy look, "New toy."

Then in a more serious tone he said, "May I speak with Officer Blackburn. This is Officer Parker calling." Turning to Sarah, he whispered, "My old title seems to get me places I can never get as a civilian."

Once the probation officer was on the phone, they chatted informally for a few minutes about the progress, or lack thereof, on the case.

"Okay, Charles. What can I do for you?" Blackburn asked.

"Our local department has some questions about Greyson. Do you know where he went and how he's traveling?"

"Unfortunately, we have no idea."

"How do you know he left town?"

"My information came to me by an informal route, but it's probably reliable. Greyson has a friend here in the department. They've been seeing each other since he was released, and she seems to be really good for him. We all thought he was getting his act together until this happened. Anyway, she told me that he left town suddenly. He told her he had *unfinished business* to take care of and promised to be back. She pleaded with me not to report his absence to the Parole Board, and I've honored her request so far, but I can't continue now that I know he may be in trouble in another jurisdiction."

"Does she know how he was traveling?"

"She had assumed he was driving, but his car is here."

"Have you checked on rentals?"

"Charlie, as I said, I was honoring her request, and I just might be in hot water over this. I haven't done anything as far as tracking the man. I've been trusting Gloria that he'll be back. Sometimes I can be a damned fool when it comes to women. She shed these big crocodile tears, and that's always the end for me."

"Me too," Charles responded, winking at Sarah. "Me too."

In a more serious tone, Charles said, "Okay. Where do we go from here?"

"I'll check the rental car companies. They're accustomed to hearing from me. If he rented a car, I'll soon know it. I'll also check the airlines. Any other ideas?"

"Maybe talk with this Gloria and see if she knows what this *unfinished business* is"

"Okay."

Then Charles added, "Oh, and if you find someone who rented him a car, see if they can locate the car's current location. They all have GPS built in now, don't they?"

"Good point. I'll get some guys on it right away."

"Thanks, Sam. Call me on this number the minute you hear anything."

"You got it," and Blackburn hung up.

"I'll never get used to you men on the telephone. Don't you ever say 'goodbye' to each other?"

"We don't want to look wimpy," he responded, trying to look serious but chuckling as he wrapped his arms around her waist.

Chapter 35

"Let's go for a walk," Sarah said cheerfully to Barney, expecting him to grab his leash off the hook. Barney raised his head but didn't move. "Come on, fella. Let's go." Still nothing.

Sarah lifted him out of his bed and placed him on the floor next to the leash, but as she reached to hook it onto his collar he returned to his bed and laid his nose against the kitty.

"It's too cold for the kitty to go out," Sarah explained to a dog who couldn't comprehend her words. She, on the other hand, completely understood what he was saying. He had no intention of leaving his new charge at home.

Charles had gone home, and the house felt empty without him. He said he had some laundry to run and would do it while he waited for Blackburn to call back. She invited him for dinner, but he said he would be back long before that.

The phone rang and she hoped it was Charles, but it was Jenny. She and Jason had called several times a day to see if there was any news. "Still nothing," Sarah responded, "but it's beginning to look like the person who took her was her ex-husband, Greyson. Everyone else seems to have legitimate alibis for that day."

"Have they found him?"

"Not yet." While they talked, Sarah pushed Barney out the back door, hoping he would not only take care of his business but also would run around and get some exercise. Unfortunately, he was back and scratching at the door a few minutes later. She let him in and, after hanging up, told him he was absolutely going for a long walk as soon as Charles arrived.

He wagged his tail when he heard the word *Charles* and returned to the warmed quilt where Bootsy was playing with her tail. As soon as he curled up, she began the long climb up his back and across to his ears. She discovered that if she tapped one with her paw it would twitch. She found this intriguing and continued to do it until he shook his head and she came tumbling down, landing by his paw. He stared at her, probably realizing this little bundle of fur wasn't as helpless as he had originally thought.

The phone rang again and this time it was Amanda. "Is Charles there?" she asked.

"No, but you can reach him on his cell. Do you have any news?"

"Actually, yes. Jillian was better after having her stomach pumped. There weren't many pills left in the bottle. I was able to talk with her this morning and, as we were beginning to suspect, she was Martha's stalker."

"Why would she do that?" Sarah asked, finding the concept incomprehensible. "Why would one woman want to terrorize another like that?"

"Jealousy. It's usually about jealousy. She was convinced Martha was having an affair with her husband. Alan came in the room right after I talked with her, and she pleaded with him to forgive her. She said she was convinced he was going to leave her."

"Is something wrong with the woman?"

"She certainly has emotional problems, but from what she told me, and if it's even true, this is something Alan has done in the past. She is suspicious of everyone he spends time with. Alan denied it to me, but who knows where the truth lies."

"Will she be prosecuted for stalking?"

"I don't think so, Sarah. She stayed on public streets and never approached Martha. Maybe your daughter could get a restraining order, but even that is doubtful. I don't think Martha will have anything to worry about. In fact, Alan is talking about transferring to the New York office."

"For Martha's sake, I hope he does," Sarah replied.

* * * * *

"Hi, sweetie," Charles called out to Sarah as he walked in the door without knocking. "Oh," he said, looking back at the door and appearing to be concerned.

"That's fine, Charles. No need to knock," she responded, assuming that was the source of his concern.

"It should be locked," he said under his breath as he walked back to set the dead bolt.

"It's open for a reason, Charles. Sophie is on her way over." Locking the door had been a bone of contention from the first day Charles visited. Sarah was accustomed to living in a safe neighborhood before she moved to Cunningham

Village and was now living with a security gate and staff who patrolled the streets.

Charles, on the other hand, spent his career working with criminals and the victims of crime. Their perspectives were totally different. It was one issue, however, about which Sarah was willing to compromise. After numerous clashes, she realized that his motivation was simply her safety. She now locked the door, even when she was home, and took the emergency key out from under the flowerpot.

"Sorry," he responded and unlocked the door just as Sophie was coming up the walk.

Once Sophie was settled at the kitchen table and Sarah had poured coffee and pulled the freshly baked cherry pie out of the oven, Charles announced, "You got here just in time, Sophie. I was just about to tell Sarah what Blackburn had to say."

"Oh! You heard from him!" Sarah exclaimed.

"Who's Blackburn?" Sophie asked.

"Greyson's parole officer," Sarah responded eager to hear what Charles had to say. "And Greyson is …"

"I know. I know. What do you think? I'm an old, demented woman?"

Ignoring her comment, Sarah turned to Charles, "What did he have to say? Does he know where Greyson is?"

"Not yet. Greyson didn't fly out of Billings, and there's no record of him renting a car. His car was located near the bus station, so we assume he left by bus."

"What's next?" Sarah asked, looking disappointed.

"Blackburn talked to the girlfriend again, and she admitted she heard from him yesterday. He didn't say where he was, but he expected to be back home this week."

Sarah said reluctantly, "What does that mean? He's taking her back to Billings, or …" She stopped talking and covered her mouth with the back of her hand. Her eyes grew large and frightened. "Oh, Charles. Is he going to kill her?"

"Sarah, we can't assume anything. He may not even be here. I told Blackburn to go back to the car rental guys. Maybe he rented the car under another name."

"Wouldn't he need identification?"

"True, but remember he's a criminal. There *are* ways."

The three picked at their pies, but none had any appetite. Suddenly Sophie jumped out of her chair sending her cane flying across the room. She screamed frantically, "What's that creature on Barney's back? A rat?"

"It's okay," Charles said, jumping up to help her back into her chair before she fell. Sarah retrieved the cane and took it to her.

"That's not a rat, Sophie." She picked up the little kitten and carried it to Sophie's chair. "See, it's a kitten. Barney found her and we brought her home." She laid the kitten in Sophie's lap. Sophie sputtered a bit and acted annoyed, but she patted the kitten's little back tenderly as Sarah was picking her up.

Barney kept his eyes on Bootsy and wagged his tail when he saw that Sarah was returning her to their quilt.

After Sophie left, Charles and Sarah decided to take Barney out for some fresh air. "Do you think it's too cold to walk to the fabric store? When Martha is back home, I'd like to make a little quilt for Bootsy." Sarah made a conscious effort to say *when Martha is back home*, trying not to acknowledge, even to herself, that it might never happen.

"It's cold. Why don't I drive us to the north side of the park. We can walk to Stitches from there. That way Barney can get some exercise, and we won't freeze." Again, with Barney strongly objecting about leaving the cat, they gently pushed him out the front door and into the car. He looked out the back window until his home was long out of sight. Once they parked and started walking, he immediately got with the program and trotted along by their side with his head and tail held high.

Ruth had taken the day off, but Anna was working in the shop. She met Sarah at the door, looking worried. "Has there been any word about your daughter?" she asked, giving Sarah a sympathetic look. "I've been so worried."

Sarah wrapped her fingers protectively around the cell phone in her pocket. "Nothing yet," she responded looking toward Charles. "You have your cell phone with you, right?"

"Yes, sweetie. I have it right here." As he patted his chest pocket, Sarah realized she had asked him the same question as they were leaving the house. She smiled, appreciating his patience.

Once she caught Anna up on what they knew about Martha's disappearance, she told her about the new kitten and her intention to make a small quilt. Anna suggested she use flannel so it would be soft and cuddly. Together they went into Ruth's flannel section, and Sarah pulled down a bolt of flannel with baby kittens in pinks and yellows. Anna reached for the fat quarter box and suggested that Sarah cut four-inch squares from several different fabrics for the quilt top and that she use the kitten flannel for the back. Sarah loved the idea and together they figured out that she would need four or five fat quarters for the top and a yard and half from the bolt for the back and the binding.

"That's going to make a pretty big quilt," Sarah said frowning. "She's only this big," she added holding her hand out to indicate the kitten would fit in her hand.

"Just wait! They grow up fast," Anna responded. "Do you have batting?"

"Yes, plenty. But how should I quilt it?"

"Why don't you tie it using long strands of embroidery floss? Your kitty will love playing with the loose ends." Anna showed her how to make the knot for a tied quilt, and they chose a multicolored skein that complemented the fabric. As Anna was ringing up the sale, Charles moved closer and pulled out his wallet.

"Not this time, Charles. I'll pay here. I have other plans for your money," she added with a smile. As they left the shop, she turned to the right and led them up the street to the pet store.

"And why are we here?" he asked as they reached the door.

"Toys! Every little girl needs toys." Charles smiled and looked down at Barney. "Is he allowed in the store?"

Sarah pointed to the sign on the door. "Leashed animals of all kinds welcome."

Once they were inside, Barney became somewhat difficult to handle. He tried to drag Charles to the birdcages, but on the way he spotted the kittens. He began to whine and bark in his pleading way.

"No, Barney. One cat is all we can handle," Sarah called to him. "Come help me pick out a kitty bed."

By the time Charles wrestled Barney over to the opposite side of the store, Sarah was already holding a tiny pink fur bed and had a pleased smile on her face. Suddenly her cell phone rang, and the blood drained from her face giving her a pallor that frightened Charles.

"Are you okay?" he asked before she could answer the phone.

Nodding to him, she pushed *Talk* and said, "Hello?"

When she heard the words, "Hi, Mom," her heart seemed to stop, but then she realized it was Jason's wife calling. Jennifer rarely called Sarah "Mom" but had been saying it more the past few days. Generally, it was fine with Sarah, but right now she yearned to hear those words from her daughter.

"Hi, Jenny." She listened for a few moments, then responded, "No, there's still no word. I'll call you the minute I hear anything." After she hung up, she leaned against Charles, and her voice cracked as she said, "I thought it was Martha."

"I know," he responded, holding her close.

Once she got her emotions under control, she returned to the shelf of cat beds and pulled out the pink fur bed. "Isn't this adorable?"

"Yes, it's certainly cute. But, as Anna pointed out, your kitten will be hanging over the sides in a few months."

"True," she responded reluctantly, returning the bed to the shelf.

He picked up another bed, still pink and feminine but larger. "This should work."

"Okay," she said doubtfully, then added, "I could make her a pillow to use up some of the extra space so she'll feel cozy. Let's take a look at the toys."

They picked out several small toys that seemed like things that would appeal to the playful kitten. Two had feathers, two were little critters, and one included a small scratching post that the sales person said she would be interested in very soon.

As they were walking toward the cash register, Sarah noticed that Barney was trotting along with his head held high in the air and a long knotted rope in his mouth. He appeared to be smiling. Sarah tapped Charles on the arm and pointed toward Barney.

"Ah, the trials of having a large family," he responded, pulling out his wallet as the young man rang up their purchases, including the long knotted rope.

Chapter 36

A s they were approaching the house, Charles' cell phone rang. He reached for it and pulled over to the curb. "Parker," he answered.

"Hey, Charlie. I think we got him!" Officer Blackburn sounded confident.

"*Great*," Charles responded. "Tell me what's going on." Charles hit the speaker button on his cell phone so Sarah could hear. "I'm putting you on speaker. I have the victim's mother here with me." He introduced the two and then said, "Go on, Tom."

"We followed your suggestion and checked out car rentals that might have used falsified identification. We found a Jonathan Harvey whose identification indicated that he would be ninety-eight years old. They called their night staff and were assured no one had rented a car to anyone that old. We checked it out, and Mr. Harvey died two years ago."

"And I assume no one could describe the guy that rented the car since they didn't even look at the identification."

"Right," Blackburn responded.

"What kind of car did they put the fake Mr. Harvey in?"

"He's in an SUV, a white Chevy Tahoe, and the GPS has him in Middletown."

"That's got to be Greyson. Is he on the move?" Charles asked.

"No. He's been in one spot for several days. He's in the Sleep-A-Way motel out on your Route 39." Charles grabbed his notebook and jotted down a few notes. "I'll call the precinct and get someone out there. Thanks, Tom."

"Thank you, Tom," Sarah called out as Charles was disconnecting. She had become both excited and agitated. "What shall we do?"

"We'll call Amanda." He dialed her number and was relieved when she answered the phone. He told her what he had learned from Blackburn, and she said she would get officers out there right away. You stay put," she added, knowing he had Sarah in the car. "I'll call you when I know something."

"I want to go!" Sarah demanded after he completed the call.

"Absolutely not," Charles responded. "There could be a shoot-out, or any number of other things might happen. It's no place for a civilian."

"But my daughter is there," she wailed.

"How about this. I'll take you and Barney home. Then I'll go to the motel to make sure Martha is safe, and I'll bring her back home to you. Is that okay?"

Sarah thought for a moment and finally agreed. If she couldn't be there, at least Charles would be. He dropped her at her house and told her to call Sophie and Jason and tell them to come to the house. "We'll have something to celebrate!" He hoped that was true but, if not, he didn't want Sarah to be alone.

It was at least a twenty-minute drive to the motel on the outskirts of town. He hoped he could get there by the time Amanda and the officers arrived.

* * * * *

Martha heard a car pull up outside the motel room. She heard muffled words and the car pulled away as quickly as it arrived. She heard heavy steps walk toward the office. *That must have been a cab*, she thought. She had given up all hope of someone coming for her. No one knew where she was.

A few minutes later she heard the heavy footsteps return. The man who said to call him *Tony* was engrossed in the television and hadn't noticed the sounds outside. He laughed at the news stories about Martha and how far off they were as they speculated about her disappearance.

Martha's wrists hurt from the rope binding them. She was stiff and wanted to move around but didn't want to draw attention to herself. He seemed to have temporarily forgotten about her. Her eyes burned with unshed tears that she couldn't wipe away.

Suddenly the door burst open. Through her tears, she saw a tall, muscular man standing in the doorway. "You sick bastard!" he screamed at her captor. "What are you doing with *my wife*?" Martha squeezed her eyes tight to clear the tears and looked up into the man's face.

"Greyson?"

The man called Tony stood and faced Greyson. "She's not your wife anymore, man. Get out!"

Without a word, Greyson instantly had the man down and began beating him in the face. Blood splattered and the man moaned. Greyson dragged him into the bathroom, tossing him in like a rag doll. He locked the door, checking first to make sure there was no escape. He immediately untied Martha who sat on the floor dazed. "How did you know where I was?" she asked.

"That fool in the bathroom has loose lips. It's no wonder he's spent most of his life in prison. He can't keep his mouth shut."

"What do you mean?" She rubbed her sore wrists and tried to get up but didn't have the strength. Greyson reached under her arms and lifted her effortlessly onto the bed. She still appeared to be in shock.

"That jerk was my cellmate. He used to drool over your pictures and always wanted me to tell him stories about you. I never thought much about it, just the ramblings of an idiot who's been away from women too long."

Martha waited for him to continue. His blond curls were beginning to gray, but she could still see the handsome boy she had fallen in love with behind his now aged and hardened face. Despite fearing him for years and hating what he had done to her, he had come to her rescue, and she couldn't help but be thankful.

"Thank you," she mumbled hesitantly. "How did you know?"

"My parole officer clued me in that this jerk was talking about marrying you. It sounded like crazy talk to both of us, but then I heard he was planning to come get you and that he was going to take you out to Oklahoma. I still figured it was all talk, but he was telling everyone about it."

Martha sat dazed. "He told me he was taking me somewhere out west, but ..."

The man locked in the bathroom began to curse, and Greyson opened the door and looked down at him on the floor. "Shut up," he said, giving him a warning kick in the ribs. "I'm deciding what to do with you."

Martha heard sirens in the background, and within seconds, cars were screeching to a stop outside the room. Again, the door burst open and three police officers entered, wearing protective gear and pointing firearms at the two. Charles came in behind them and cried out, "Stop! That's Martha." He leaned down and wrapped his arms around her, lifting her off the bed and half carried her out to Amanda's squad car. Amanda jumped out of the car and hurried around to help him get her into the car.

"Are you hurt?" she asked. "We have an ambulance on the way."

"He didn't hurt me," she responded, still rubbing her wrists and beginning to cry with relief. "Just a little rope burn."

"After an EMT takes a look at you, I'm going to take you to your mother's house, and we'll talk there after we get him locked up. Is he still in the room?"

"Yes. Greyson subdued him and locked him in the bathroom."

"*Greyson?*" Amanda and Charles said in unison.

"Greyson subdued *who*? Wasn't Greyson the one who kidnapped you?"

"No. It was a man named Tony. Greyson knew him."

"So what is Greyson doing here?" Charles asked. "Was he in on your kidnapping?"

"No. Greyson found out what this guy was up to, and he came here to stop him. He was almost too late...." She began crying, mostly out of relief.

The EMT arrived and checked her out, but she refused to go to the hospital. She just wanted to go home.

Amanda spoke briefly with the officers and returned to the car. "They're taking Greyson in for questioning, and we'll talk to Montana about whether they want him arrested. He's violated parole, but then he has a reasonable excuse. He might need you to testify for him," she added, looking at Martha. Martha thought about that time years ago when she was terrified of testifying against him, and now, years later, she might be testifying *for* him. She smiled at the irony.

"And his parole officer just might cut him some slack." Charles said, smiling as he thought about how far out on a limb Blackburn had gone for Greyson.

"What about that guy Tony?" Martha asked cautiously. "He'll be locked up, right?"

"He'll be in the prison hospital for a day or two and then charged," Amanda responded. "Montana will probably wait to see what happens to him here. He's jumped parole there, but we have him on assault, false imprisonment, possibly kidnapping. They'll put a retainer on him, so he'll be sent back to them when we're through with him. The guy won't see the light of day for many years," she added with a chuckle as she walked back toward the motel room. "You folks wait there."

Once the prisoners were taken away, Amanda walked her partner to his car, and they talked for a few minutes before he drove off. She then returned to her car. Martha was leaning against Charles, and he had a protective arm around her shoulder. "Put your seat belts on, folks. We're headed home."

As she drove, Amanda leaned her head back to speak to Martha. "It looks like he brought you here sometime on Thursday. I'm glad you were still here in town, but what was he waiting for?"

"He asked me if I had any money. That's when I got the idea. I told him Mom has lots of money and that we should wait until she gets back from Chicago. I convinced him she would give us as much as we wanted." Charles looked surprised that she would involve her mother, but Martha, sensing his concern, added, "I was worried about bringing her into it, but I was sure you two would be involved by then. I knew you would figure out what was happening. I was taking a chance, but this guy was a loose cannon, and I didn't want him to leave the city with me."

"Good thinking, gal. Good thinking."

"How did you find me?"

"Your stalker saw the guy grab you in front of your house."

"*My stalker?*" Martha responded looking confused.

Charles told her about Jillian Fitzgerald. "Alan's wife?" she exclaimed with disbelief. "Why in the world would she be stalking *me*?"

"The green-eyed monster. She was obsessively jealous of you and Alan. She was sure you two were having an affair, and she followed you incessantly, determined to catch you."

"Why would she think that?"

"Well, she was right about one thing. He *was* having an affair. And if she hadn't spent all her time following you, she might have actually caught him with the *right* person." He looked at her with a sly look as if he knew something she just might like to know.

"And who might that be?" she asked coyly, willing to play his game now that she was safe and on her way home.

"Your pretty blond administrative assistant!"

"Sheila?"

"You bet. And guess who's been feeding Alan's wife with all the false information about Alan and you?"

"*Sheila?*"

"Right again! And she even gave Jillian the key to your house so she could look for proof of the nonexistent affair!"

"I wonder …" Martha began.

"I know what you are wondering, and you are partially right! Now, she wasn't the actual corporate mole. She's not that smart. The mole was some computer jerk in Davis' lab, but our little blond friend, Sheila, was feeding information to him as well."

"Why would she do all this?"

"Your mother suspects that Sheila's in love with Alan and was doing everything she could to discredit you and break up his marriage," Charles explained.

Amanda, in the front seat, was listening to the entire conversation and smiling. "Your mom is one smart puppy!"

Chapter 37

"They're here," Sarah shouted, rushing out the front door. She had been elated since Charles called her from the motel to tell her Martha was safe. She spoke to her daughter briefly, but their sobs of joy were so intense that they could barely understand one another.

"Wait! Put your coat on," Sophie called after her. "It's freezing out there!" Tim grabbed Sarah's coat and quickly followed her toward the squad car. Charles hopped out and ran around the car to open the door for Martha. Amanda got out and smiled at Sarah who was hurrying toward the car with Tim right behind her trying to help her on with her coat as she walked.

"Slow down," he said. "I can't get your arm in!"

"Mama!" Martha cried out. She ran into her mother's arms and they both laughed and cried simultaneously.

"You're safe," Sarah whispered in her daughter's ear. "You're safe now!"

As the group walked toward the house, Sophie appeared at the door wiping her hands on the apron Sarah had loaned her. "Get in this house before you all freeze," she demanded, looking stern despite the tears that had welled up in her eyes. She reached out and gently patted Martha's shoulder.

"Welcome home, honey." She said. "Come on in and curl up in one of your mother's quilts. I'll fix you a nice cup of hot cocoa." As always, Sophie was ready with her usual solution to life's stresses—food. She had baked two enormous apple tarts while they were waiting for Charles and Martha. The aroma of freshly brewed coffee wafted from the kitchen. The teapot was threatening to whistle at any moment, and warmed milk for cocoa was steaming on the stove.

Amanda seemed to be hesitant about following them into the house, but Sarah called to her, "Come on in, Amanda. You're part of this reunion."

"Thank you, Sarah," she responded somewhat reticently. As she got closer to Sarah, she added softly, "I hate to say this, but I need to get some information from Martha. Do you mind if I take her aside for just a few minutes? Then I can call my partner at the station with these last few details. He offered to do the paperwork so I could be here with you folks.

"Absolutely. Let's get that out of the way first. Why don't you use the guest room. There're several chairs in there and the futon in case Martha wants to lay down." Turning to Martha who already had a quilt around her shoulders, Sarah said, "Amanda needs to talk with you for a few minutes. You two can use the guest room."

Martha smiled weakly, dreading having to go over the details, but she knew it was necessary. "I'll be right there," she called to Amanda, stopping first to hug Charles and whisper, "Thank you, Charles. You're the best."

"I love you, sweetie. Now, go take care of business so we can all relax."

Once Martha finished talking with Amanda and relaxed for a while with her family and friends, Sarah asked her if she wanted to go home. She was afraid that all the commotion was too much for her. "I'll take you home if you would rather be there. You must be exhausted," Sarah said, hoping Martha would refuse the offer.

"I'm exhausted, that's for sure. But, I'm also very relaxed. I really don't want to be alone just yet."

"Do you want me to stay with you for a day or two?" Sarah asked. "I could ..."

Martha interrupted her mother saying, "I would love to just stay here for a few days if it's okay with you. I feel so safe here."

Sarah grinned and sat down next to Martha on the couch, slipping her arm around her daughter's shoulder. "I would love to have you stay here with me for as long as you want to stay!" She looked at Charles, and he knew she was overjoyed at the idea of having her daughter home with her.

Later that afternoon, the doorbell rang and Jennifer walked in followed by Jason carrying little Alaina. "I need to give my sister a hug," Jason said handing the baby to Sarah.

A few minutes later, the doorbell rang again. This time, a young boy stood there holding a pile of pizza boxes. Charles hurried to the door and handed the boy some bills. "Dinner is served," he announced, heading for the kitchen with his pizza boxes.

Holding her granddaughter close to her heart, Sarah looked around the room. She had her entire family and her most precious friends all in one room. After a few long days of worried desperation, she felt nothing but love and joy.

* * * * *

Later that evening, Sarah walked out of the kitchen wearing a mischievous smile. Charles was right behind her with a bottle of red wine in one hand and white in the other. "Who's ready for a refill?" he asked with the grin of a proud Cheshire cat spread across his face.

He turned toward Sarah and asked, "Shall we?" She nodded.

Turning to the group, Sarah announced, "We'd like for all our friends and family to join us on New Year's Eve for a gala party." She hesitated for a moment, and then added, "We'll be celebrating the New Year at the community center with music and dancing, a catered dinner, champagne, and," Sarah added with a happy glow, "… a midnight wedding!"

The cheer that went up in the room could be heard up and down the block.

See full quilt on back cover.

MEMORIES OF HOME

PROJECT

The Friday Night Quilters loved the idea of making an Amish quilt for Ruth. This 61″ × 72¼″ quilt, with its combination of black and solids, is a classic example of the Amish style.

MATERIALS

Assorted solid colors: To total 4½ yards

Black: 3¼ yards (⅞ yard for blocks, ½ yard for inner border, 1¼ yards for outer border, ⅝ yard for binding)

Middle border: ⅓ yard

Backing: 3⅞ yards

Batting: 69″ × 80″

Project Instructions

Seam allowances are ¼". WOF = width of fabric.

MAKE THE BLOCKS

1. For 1 block, cut 6 strips 2⅜" × 6", 3 strips each from a light and a dark fabric. (For multiple same-color blocks, see Step 5.)

2. Sew together 2 strip sets of 3 strips each, alternating light and dark: 1 set of light-dark-light strips and another set of dark-light-dark strips. Press toward the dark.

3. Cut the strip sets into 2⅜" sections.

4. Sew together 3 sections, matching the light to the dark and nesting the seams. Press.

5. Follow Steps 1–4 to make the number of blocks you need for any colorway. For example, 5 green/pink blocks multiplied by 6" requires 30"-long strips. Make a total of 80 blocks in any color combinations you want.

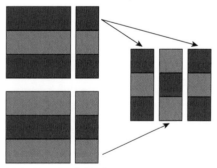

Make Nine-Patch blocks.

MAKE THE BORDERS

1. For the inner border: Cut 6 strips 2⅜″ × WOF. Join the strips end to end. Press. Subcut 2 strips 2⅜″ × 56¾″ for the sides and 2 strips 2⅜″ × 49¼″ for the top and bottom.

2. For the middle border: Cut 6 strips 1⅝″ × WOF. Join the strips end to end. Press. Subcut 2 strips 1⅝″ × 60½″ for the sides and 2 strips 1⅝″ × 51½″ for the top and bottom.

3. For the outer border: Cut 7 strips 5½″ × WOF. Join the strips end to end. Press. Subcut 2 strips 5½″ × 62¾″ for the sides and 2 strips 5½″ × 61½″ for the top and bottom.

ASSEMBLE AND FINISH THE QUILT

1. Sew 8 blocks together into a row. Press. Make 10 rows.

2. Sew the rows together. Press.

3. Sew the inner borders to each side. Press. Sew the inner borders to the top and bottom. Press.

4. Sew the middle borders to each side. Press. Sew the middle borders to the top and bottom. Press.

5. Sew the outer borders to each side. Press. Sew the outer borders to the top and bottom. Press.

6. Layer the pieced top with batting and backing. Quilt and bind as desired.

Turn the page for a preview ---------------------------→ *of the next book in A Quilting Cozy series.*

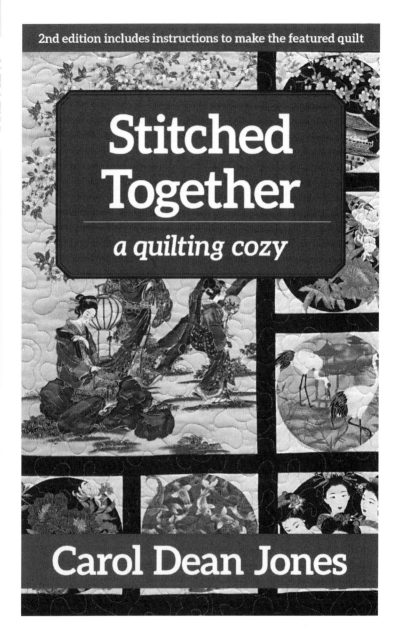

2nd edition includes instructions to make the featured quilt

Stitched Together

a quilting cozy

Carol Dean Jones

Preview of
Stitched Together

It was drizzling the day they arrived in Paris. Charles held the umbrella, and Sarah gripped his arm, snuggling against him as they walked. "I'm glad we waited until now," she said, looking up at her husband of four months with a twinkle in her eye.

Charles wrapped his arm around her and pulled her even closer. "I'm just glad we're finally here." They'd been planning their honeymoon for several months but had decided to wait for warm weather. They were married during one of the worst snowstorms the Midwest had seen for years and decided it was no time to be at the mercy of the airlines.

It was early spring and, despite the light rain, Sarah found Paris to be breathtaking.

Earlier that day, they had taken a cab from the airport to their hotel in Montmartre. The driver offered to give them a quick sightseeing tour through the downtown area and past the Louvre; along the way, he pointed out popular shops, the museums, and bridges crossing the Seine to the Left Bank.

Their hotel was situated above the city, halfway up the hill leading to the Sacré-Coeur. From their fifth-floor window, Sarah could look out over the rooftops of the city. "What an awesome view," she exclaimed when Charles joined her at the window. Their room was spacious and comfortably decorated, although they knew they probably wouldn't spend much time there considering all the sightseeing they had planned.

Sarah picked up a brochure that described several nearby restaurants and cafés, along with a list of things to do in Paris and a street map. But after scanning the brochure, she realized that ten days might not be enough time to see all the things they hoped to see.

After getting settled and freshened up, they left the hotel on foot. Glancing down at the map she was carrying, Sarah commented, "Paris is much smaller than I realized. I think we can walk to most things."

"It's not quite that small, but we can use the metro and cabs," he responded. "How about grabbing some lunch?" Charles asked cheerfully as he picked up the pace.

"Hey! I'm taking three steps for every one of yours," she teased. "Slow down!"

"Sorry," he responded, pulling her close and attempting to adapt to her pace.

"And," she added, "I don't think one *grabs lunch* in Paris. I believe the French have developed the art of savoring their meals."

They stopped at a café up the street from their hotel and were led to a small round table near the window. Charles reached across the table and took her hand. "Are you happy?"

"Ecstatic!" Sarah giggled with the excitement of a child at a theme park. "But I'm trying to act my age," she added, attempting to present a demeanor more in keeping with her years. *Seventy years old and a blushing bride*, she thought. Her face became flushed at the thought.

It had been twenty years since her husband, Jonathan, had died, and she had become accustomed to her life as a widow. A few years ago, she had retired and moved to a retirement community, Cunningham Village, where she made friends, learned to quilt, and was enjoying her independence. And then she met Charles.

Charles was a detective, retired from the local police department. A serious stroke brought him to Cunningham Village, where he spent many months in their rehab center before settling into one of their apartments that offered assisted living. He no longer needed special services and was totally independent when he met Sarah, but he had decided to continue living in the community. He fell in love with Sarah the day they met.

In fact, Charles would tell you he fell in love with her long before that. He was the police officer who notified Sarah that her husband had suffered a fatal accident on the job. Charles never forgot this lovely, gentle woman, but she had been too grief-stricken to be aware of him back then.

"Look!" Sarah exclaimed, pointing toward the sky. "It's stopped raining, and I think the sun's coming out."

"What would you like to do today?" Charles asked as the waitress was serving their drinks.

"I'd like to walk. I want to get to know Paris, and there's no better way! Let's start with the Sacré-Coeur." Handing him the map she added, "It's only a short walk from here, and it overlooks the city."

"It's a short walk, *all uphill*," Charles responded with a chuckle.

"But then it's *downhill* coming back," she replied with a reassuring twinkle in her eye.

The young waitress arrived with their lunches and refilled their wine glasses from the decanter of chardonnay that had been placed between them. Charles had ordered Provençal slow-roasted pork and *pommes frites*, which he later learned was a very fancy way of saying french fries. Sarah, wanting to experience something new, ordered a goat cheese salad served with raspberry honey dressing and a French baguette. "No escargot?" Charles asked teasingly.

"Not yet, but I'll get there before the week is over." The couple enjoyed a relaxed meal, savoring the food and enjoying the atmosphere.

"Are you ready to climb the hill?" she asked as they left the café.

"Ready and able," he responded, pulling the map out of his breast pocket. "I think we should head up past that cemetery and pick up Rue de la Bonne. It looks like that street goes right up to the Basilica." As they walked along the cobblestone sidewalk, signs confirmed that they had chosen well. Suddenly the narrow cobblestone road took a left turn and opened up at the foot of the Sacré-Coeur Basilica, which loomed high above them.

"Magnificent!" Sarah gasped, not prepared for the splendor of the architecture. As they climbed the multitude of steps up to the portico, they both became very quiet, respecting the sacredness of their surroundings. Once inside, they sat in the opulent sanctuary and held hands without speaking. Sarah had tears in her eyes as they walked to the marble steps leading up to the dome.

Looking out over Paris, Sarah revised her earlier statement. "I guess it's not as small as I thought it was," she said, gazing over the mass of rooftops spreading out in all directions. "Is that the Seine I see over there, just beyond the Eiffel Tower?" she asked, pointing toward what appeared to be water snaking through the city.

"Yes, and I want to spend our last night in Paris drifting down the Seine on a romantic dinner cruise," Charles said, pulling her close to him.

Sarah nodded enthusiastically adding, "And I want to walk across the bridges in the rain like they do in the movies!"

Charles laughed. "And I'll sing and dance with a cane and a top hat!"

By the time they returned to their hotel room, neither was interested in walking over a bridge or anywhere else. Their feet hurt from their new shoes, and Charles' arthritis in his right hip was causing him discomfort. They had dinner sent up to their room, and they stretched out on the bed watching *The Expendables*, with Arnold Schwarzenegger speaking French. Charles seemed to be enjoying it. As Sarah turned over and closed her eyes, she muttered, "You owe me one *chick flick*."

Before they knew it, they were on the plane flying home, leaving Paris and their many adventures far behind them. They couldn't believe how fast the days flew by. They were sad to see their honeymoon end, but they were both eager to return to their new life as *Mr. and Mrs. Parker*.

Had they known what was in store for them, they wouldn't have been so eager.

A Note from the Author

I hope you enjoyed *Patchwork Connections* as much as I enjoyed writing it. This is the fourth book in A Quilting Cozy Series and is followed by *Stitched Together*, which finds the friends pulling together to save one of their own.

On page 218, I have included a preview to *Stitched Together* so that you can get an idea of what our cast of characters will be involved in next.

Please let me know how you are enjoying this series. I love hearing from my readers and encourage you to contact me on my blog or send me an email.

Best wishes,

Carol Dean Jones
caroldeanjones.com
quiltingcozy@gmail.com

READER'S GUIDE:
A QUILTING COZY SERIES
by Carol Dean Jones

1. Consider how the title of this book relates to the content. How did the many connections that were made between the characters change their lives? Consider the connections between Sophie and her son, Sarah and her daughter, Martha and Tim, and Sarah and Charles.

2. How do you think Sarah's independent nature and Charles' need to protect those he loves will affect their relationship? Is a long-term relationship destined to fail? Why or why not?

3. For most of her life, Martha chose to isolate herself, keeping her problems to herself. She claimed she was protecting her family, but it becomes clear that perhaps she was simply afraid to risk relationships. What factors helped her learn to reach out to friends and family? Do you think Sarah's strong independent streak is a milder version of this fear?

4. Greyson had been a cruel and abusive husband. What do you think caused him to risk his own position with the parole board in order to attempt to save Martha from harm?

5. Why do you think everyone assumed the stalker was a man?

A Quilting Cozy Series by Carol Dean Jones